You're About to Become a

Privileged Woman.

INTRODUCING
PAGES & PRIVILEGES™.

It's our way of thanking you for buying
our books at your favorite retail store.

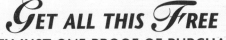

— *GET ALL THIS FREE* —

WITH JUST ONE PROOF OF PURCHASE:

◆ **Hotel Discounts up to 60% at home and abroad**

◆ **Travel Service - Guaranteed lowest published airfares plus 5% cash back on tickets**

◆ **$25 Travel Voucher**

◆ **Sensuous Petite Parfumerie collection ($50 value)**

◆ **Insider Tips Letter with sneak previews of upcoming books**

◆ **Mystery Gift (if you enroll before 6/15/95)**

You'll get a FREE personal card, too.
It's your passport to all these benefits– and to
even more great gifts & benefits to come!

There's no club to join. No purchase commitment. No obligation.

As a *Privileged Woman,* you'll be entitled to all these *Free Benefits.* And *Free Gifts,* too.

To thank you for buying our books, we've designed an exclusive FREE program called *PAGES & PRIVILEGES™*. You can enroll with just one Proof of Purchase, and get the kind of luxuries that, until now, you could only read about.

*B*IG HOTEL DISCOUNTS

A privileged woman stays in the finest hotels. And so can you—at up to 60% off! Imagine standing in a hotel check-in line and watching as the guest in front of you pays $150 for the same room that's only costing you $60. Your *Pages & Privileges* discounts are good at Sheraton, Marriott, Best Western, Hyatt and thousands of other fine hotels all over the U.S., Canada and Europe.

*F*REE DISCOUNT TRAVEL SERVICE

A privileged woman is always jetting to romantic places.
When you fly, just make one phone call for the lowest published airfare at time of booking—or double the difference back! PLUS—

you'll get a $25 voucher to use the first time you book a flight AND 5% cash back on every ticket you buy thereafter through the travel service!

She was a woman, all right...

And she stood right smack in the middle of the crate he'd just opened, wearing nothing but scarves. "Who the hell—"

She threw her arms around his neck. "Thank you, master. May your descendants be blessed."

He loosened her grip and settled her cautiously on her sandaled feet. "Lady, who are you and how did you get here?"

"If you found me in that wooden box, then that is where I was." She held out her arms in a graceful gesture as though to embrace the whole of the Rockies. "The spell is finally broken."

Maybe if she'd been wearing a few more clothes, Parker would've been able to think straight. "Spell...?" His eyes narrowed. "I get it. If you stowed away in that crate, I can understand that. Lots of people want to get to the States."

"What I tell you is true, master. I have lived in that lamp—"

Parker felt the chill over his whole body. "Are—are you trying to tell me you're...a genie?"

Dear Reader,

You're about to meet Charlotte Maclay's newest—and zaniest—heroine yet! At times we've all felt out of step with the rest of the world, but Nesrin certainly has reason. And just wait until she lays eyes on that sexy single dad—cowboy Parker Dunlap! The results are truly out of this world, making this a unique HEARTBEAT.

We've been delighted by your response to the first several HEARTBEAT titles, and we hope you continue to enjoy this program of American Romance novels featuring unusual plot twists and unique characters!

Sincerely,

Debra Matteucci
Senior Editor & Editorial Coordinator
Harlequin Books
300 East 42nd St., 6th Floor
New York, NY 10017

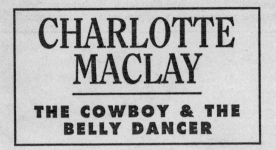

CHARLOTTE MACLAY

THE COWBOY & THE BELLY DANCER

Harlequin Books

TORONTO • NEW YORK • LONDON
AMSTERDAM • PARIS • SYDNEY • HAMBURG
STOCKHOLM • ATHENS • TOKYO • MILAN
MADRID • WARSAW • BUDAPEST • AUCKLAND

ISBN 0-373-16585-4

THE COWBOY & THE BELLY DANCER

Prologue

*Long ago in a small sheikhdom, so insignificant its
name has been lost in antiquity, a time and place of
black magic and unspeakable cruelties.*

The wizard Rasheyd sneered down his beaklike nose at
Nesrin. "Your father has lost the wager, worthless
woman. Unless you submit to me I shall condemn you
for all eternity."

"Please, have mercy, effendi." Fear constricted Nesrin's throat so tightly her words came out as little more
than a hoarse whisper. "You already have more than
enough women in your harem. What use have you for
one more insignificant female such as myself?" The
mere thought of the wizard's bony fingers touching
Nesrin's flesh, or doing even more intimate things to
her, sent a roil of nausea through her midsection.

"If you deny me that which is rightfully mine, you
shall regret your decision."

The wizard, and all the stories she'd heard of his evil
powers, terrified Nesrin. No one could counteract his

curses, certainly not her father, who was a weak magician but much beloved in her eyes. And Nesrin had few spells within her limited abilities that offered any hope of escape.

She eyed Rasheyd. Dressed in unforgiving black, his mustache curved above thin lips and a dark ring of kohl circled his eyes. A frightening sight. Even so, Nesrin sank to her knees, shaking her head as the silken veils of her skirt puddled around her on the marble floor and a shank of dark hair shifted across her shoulder. She drew a shaky breath. She would not willingly submit to such an evil man.

She shivered in the wizard's dimly lit conjuring room, a place buried so deeply beneath the sands of the Persian desert there was no hope of discovery or rescue. A pedestal made of four sun-bleached elephant tusks rested in the center of the stark space, each of the table's legs inlaid with alternating rubies and emeralds that reflected the torchlight. On the pedestal sat a brass lamp smudged with soot. Hammered inscriptions covered the lamp in an ancient script.

Panic pelted Nesrin like a desert sandstorm. If only her father had not lost such a desperate wager...

"I will give you one last chance, daughter of a hairless cur." Rasheyd's powerful voice reverberated in the small room. "Will you submit to me?"

She knew she was condemning herself to unutterable horrors. But her pride demanded that, above all else, she be true to herself. "Nay," she whispered, "I shall not submit."

He began the curse slowly. She stared at the serpentine tattoo that circled the wizard's thumb as each word etched itself into her brain with the same painful reality as acid on marble. No escape. And if she should by some miracle find release, and do the unthinkable act of submitting to another, Rasheyd would seek her out, and she would be condemned for all eternity with no further hope of redemption.

To lie with a man other than Rasheyd was forbidden. Forever. Beyond the time of the moon and stars. And if she should disobey his dictate, no one would be able to save her from the power of his curse. Doomed forever to darkness.

"So sayeth Rasheyd!"

His words stopped. The sudden silence was deafening.

A great pressure squeezed her from all directions, reshaping her insides and making her boneless. She felt herself being sucked into a narrow opening, halted only momentarily as one of her veils caught on a jagged edge and tore. Then she fell into darkness so bleak and deep, sight had no meaning.

A single proud tear crept down her cheek.

She had not submitted.

Chapter One

In the Colorado Rockies

Parker Dunlap stood at the back of his pickup and levered the lid of the wooden crate with a crowbar. Shipped from an obscure country in the Middle East, the stencils on the box declared the contents belonged to Marge and Jack Johnson, his kid sister and her husband.

The crate looked as if it had been nailed together by a drunken carpenter. Probably the same reckless driver who had left Marge's two kids orphaned, Parker thought grimly, and him in a fix because he didn't know squat about parenting.

Though he'd certainly vowed to do his darnedest with nine-year-old Kevin and his six-year-old sister, Amy. Any other option—like their grandfather taking over parenting duties—was totally unacceptable.

Using the crowbar, Parker applied additional pressure to the crate, and with a final groan of protest, the lid came loose.

Gingerly exploring the crate's contents, he found his brother-in-law's agricultural textbooks used on his teaching assignment in that remote country, some hand-embroidered linens, a couple of brass candlesticks and a battered oil lamp that Marge had probably picked up cheap at some thieves' market. He wasn't sure who had packed the crates. Friends of the family, he supposed.

Parker absently rubbed his callused thumb over the archaic inscriptions on the lamp, remembering how even as a kid Marge had loved to shop in every out-of-the-way place where their father, General Everett Dunlap, had been assigned. More than once, Parker had hauled her fanny back home when she'd ended up in a place where a young girl wouldn't be safe.

Ignoring a sheen of tears that blurred his vision, Parker stared off into the distance, past the weather-worn barns of his Colorado ranch and the restless mustangs in the corral, to the dramatically rising peaks of the Rockies. Even though he hadn't seen his sister often, their paths taking them to opposite corners of the world, he was going to miss her terribly.

From the barn came the laughter of children—kids who resembled Marge so much it made Parker ache for the one good memory from his otherwise loveless youth.

He felt the weight of the brass lamp in his hands and laughed mirthlessly. Too bad it wasn't a magic lamp that could bring Marge back to the living.

"Abracadabra," he said softly, then carelessly tossed the lamp back into the crate and turned to pry open the lid of the next box that was weighing down the back of his pickup.

"May Allah be praised!"

His head snapped up at the sound of a decidedly feminine voice.

Oh, she was a woman, all right, standing smack in the middle of the crate he'd just opened, tugging on the end of a scarf or something that seemed to be caught. A damn near naked woman!

"Who the hell—"

The piece of diaphanous silk broke free. Unbalanced, she gave a little cry that sounded like the tinkle of fine crystal, then tumbled out of the crate right into Parker's arms. He registered a whole raft of sensations at once. She couldn't weigh as much as even a small bale of hay, was as sexy as any woman he'd ever seen, had wide, expressive brown eyes and her raven hair was as dark as the inside of a Colorado silver mine.

All of that reminded Parker he hadn't had a woman in a very long time. Suddenly he wanted to correct that oversight as quickly as possible, and his body responded instantly to the thought.

Given the bizarre circumstances, however, restraint appeared to be the order of the day.

She hugged him fiercely around his neck. "Thank you, master, O great one, redeemer and all-powerful wizard, for freeing me at last. May your descendants be many times blessed. I had all but given up hope."

He loosened her grip and settled her cautiously on her sandaled feet. She wobbled a little, steadying herself by resting her small hands on his forearms. Her touch was as gentle as a summer breeze, as soft as a rose petal.

"Lady, who are you?"

"Nesrin." She smiled up at him as if that should be enough of an explanation.

It wasn't. "Nesrin what?"

"Just Nesrin. Though my beloved father, who was a great magician, sometimes called me Nessy."

"Right. So how did you get here?"

She glanced over her shoulder. "It seems the lamp in which I have been held captive for so long has traveled to this place. I am very grateful."

"The lamp?" He scowled. She couldn't mean the scuzzy brass thing he'd been messing with. That was too ridiculous to even consider. "Come on, sweetheart. How did you manage to hide in that wooden crate all the way from the Middle East?" More likely, she'd hitched a ride in the back of the truck from the airport in Colorado Springs where he'd picked up the kids that morning.

"If that is where you found the lamp, in that wooden box, then that is where I was."

"Halfway around the world in the baggage compartment of a jetliner? Where it's freezing cold and there's no oxygen?" he challenged.

"That I would not know, master. I only know that once I was somewhere else, and now I am here." She held out her arms in a graceful gesture as though to embrace the whole of the Rockies. "The wizard's spell is finally broken," she said with a sigh.

Maybe if she'd been wearing a few more clothes, Parker would have been able to think straighter. The bits of colorful silk she wore were practically see-through, and her bare midriff revealed creamy-white flesh that cried out for a man's touch.

"A spell?" he asked incredulously. Her eyes were the darkest, most innocent shade of brown he'd ever seen this side of a doe caught unaware in the headlights of his truck. A female fully capable of casting a sexual spell over an unwary male, he quickly concluded.

"Oh, yes, my father wagered that the wizard Rasheyd did not have the power to condemn anyone to the lamp." She lifted her delicate shoulders in an easy shrug of acceptance. "Rasheyd is an evil man, and very powerful."

"Your father bet..." Parker shook his head. This was not a conversation he wanted to pursue. "Nesrin—or whatever your name is—I don't believe in magic or spells, or any of that superstitious nonsense. If you stowed away in Marge's stuff, I can understand that. A lot of people want to get to the States, legally or not." Though he still couldn't imagine how she had survived the trip.

"What I tell you is true, master. I have lived in that lamp—"

"Are you trying to tell me you're a genie?"

Nesrin felt scalding heat stain her cheeks. A genie of the lowest rank, she hated to tell this great wizard with his flashing green eyes how poor her mystical skills were. If she had been gifted with decent powers, she would have cast herself out of the lamp centuries ago.

"Yes, master," she admitted softly.

"Terrific. Does that mean I get three wishes?"

"Regretfully, I am not that sort of a genie, master. I have only a few spells I can conjure."

The man who had rescued her folded his arms across his broad chest. Disbelief was written clearly in the ruggedly handsome lines of his face, and the way he narrowed his gaze. "Not that I doubt you for a minute, but how about casting some little spell to prove you're telling me the truth."

She swallowed hard. "I may be a bit out of practice."

"I'll wait."

Anxiously she glanced around to see what spell she might attempt without creating too much havoc if she failed. They were standing next to what she took to be a modern vehicle in which several wooden crates rested. One was open to reveal the lamp lying on its side. A likely target she thought. *If* she could right it.

Closing her eyes, she concentrated all of her powers on the brass lamp that had imprisoned her for so many years. She'd been so dreadfully lonely the mere thought of returning to such an existence sent a shiver of terror stroking down her spine. To have not looked on a human face in centuries, to have not seen a smile, or felt the touch of another person in all that time was cruelty beyond endurance. Only voices had reached her in the blackness, and her heart had reached back to those unseen people, but to no avail. She had learned their words but could not speak; she had cried for their sorrows and rejoiced in their triumphs, but had not been able to ease the cruel loneliness she endured.

Mentally she speared the lamp full force with her powers, determined to demonstrate she was worthy to be her father's daughter.

Air hissed loudly from somewhere nearby.

"What the heck?" the man complained.

Nesrin opened her eyes. The black wheel at the rear of the vehicle was now oddly shaped. Quite flat on the bottom, she observed, doubting it would roll well even along the smoothest of roads.

He kicked at the wheel. "A rock must have slammed against the tire and busted the stem when I was driving the kids back from the airport."

"I did not mean to hurt your wheel, master."

"Honey, just call me 'Parker.' And you didn't do anything. It's an old tire."

Nesrin did not think that was the case. As usual, her aim had been slightly off target. One would have hoped the centuries of disuse would have improved her powers, not left her with the same discouraging sense of failure. Little wonder her father had been willing to risk her future. Too many times she had embarrassed him.

Too proud to admit failure, she raised her chin. "If you would like, I will try another incantation."

"No, that's all right." He lifted his broad-brimmed hat and ran his hand across hair the color of a sand dune at dawn, the soft strands cut short to lie softly in waves against his well-shaped head. "Seems to me the best thing I could do is to get you back to where you came from."

The blood drained from Nesrin's face, pooling in her stomach and churning there like a caldron of brackish desert water. "You would send me back into the lamp?" she asked in dismay.

His very appealing lips twitched at the corners. "I don't think I've got that kind of power. But I'd guess the immigration people would like to have a chat with you."

She stared at him stupidly. "Immigration?"

"Do you have a passport, Nesrin?"

Shaking her head, she said, "I have only that which you can see."

He cleared his throat, his gaze skimming over her in a lazy, interested perusal. "All of which is very nice, I admit."

For the first time, Nesrin felt a frisson of awareness that had nothing to do with fear. The sensation started in her breasts, making them feel strangely fuller, then burrowed its way to a point much lower in her body. "Please, master...Parker," she corrected. "Do not send me away. Do not send me to where Rasheyd can find me again." For he would surely condemn her back into the lamp without so much as a second thought, so bitter had been the rivalry between the wizard and her father. Only this man named Parker seemed to have the power to match his deeds.

Parker squared his Stetson on his head. He was tempted to keep this woman around any way he could.

Nesrin had given his libido a good, hard wake-up call. But he knew about lust. A temporary urge better ignored. And he knew about women. His ex-wife had been quite a teacher. The lesson had cost him most of what he'd owned, including putting the ranch at risk, and half of his pride. Between Joyce, his truncated tour of duty in Special Forces, and years of stern discipline from his father, Parker had learned a lot. None of which he wanted to repeat. And all of which made it clear a guy with a soft heart was likely to finish last.

"Sorry, sweetheart. I don't need any more hired hands just now."

Her expression crumpled like a sand sculpture caught in the shifting tides. But before he had a chance to reconsider his decision, Amy's high-pitched giggle echoed from the barn where both she and her brother had been getting the grand tour from Parker's hired hands. A new litter of kittens had been high on the to-see list.

Nesrin turned and smiled broadly. "The children? They are here, too?"

"You know the kids?"

"Amy and Kevin? Oh, yes. I know them."

"And my sister... their parents?"

Her eyes misted over. "I cried when I heard they had been killed. I wanted to help...." She shook her head, her dark hair shifting like a silken black waterfall over her delicate shoulder.

"How did you know them?" Parker persisted.

"For these last few years, I had thought of myself as a member of their household... your sister Marge, her husband Jack and the children. They were a very happy family. The most happy I have ever lived with. Their deaths were so sad."

The pieces of the puzzle were beginning to come together a bit more clearly for Parker. Among other delightful attributes, his sister had a way of picking up strays—human or otherwise.

At that moment both kids came out of the horse barn, Amy running so fast she created her own tiny dust devil that twirled across the fenced corral, agitating the mustangs and causing the mares to nicker.

"Rusty says I can pick the litter," Amy cried. Her little legs did double time across the yard. She carried her ratty-looking doll by the hand.

"That's pick *of* the litter, and don't bug Uncle Parker all the time," Kevin complained. His tennis shoes scuffed up their own clouds of dust. He was the tough macho kind of kid with a stringy blond ponytail that needed to be whacked off and a shirttail that needed to be tucked in. "I told ya I'd asked for you, didn't I?"

From the rise of ground to the west of the barn, a stallion trumpeted his response to the mares' calls.

Parker whipped his head that direction. Bearing down on the outbuildings, and heading right for Amy, galloped the leader of the captured mustangs. The magnificent black beast had eluded the roundup and was now set on freeing his harem.

"Watch out!" Parker shouted. Waving his hat to spook the stallion, Parker made directly for Amy. He scooped her up under his arm just as the horse veered away, his heaving breath hot on Parker's collar.

Turning, he saw the horse racing toward Nesrin. She made no effort to escape, rooted to the spot by terror, he imagined.

Fear rocketed through him. She was going to be trampled.

"Get in the truck," he yelled. "Just leap into the back."

To his dismay, she still didn't give ground, her attention riveted on the horse that was bearing down on her. She was the most courageous woman he'd ever seen. Or a damn fool!

"Get out of the way!" he ordered again, knowing full well it was already too late.

"Uncle Parker..." Amy cried, burying her face in his chest.

In a circus move, Nesrin ducked at the very last instant, grabbed a handful of mane and pulled herself up onto the stallion's back. She laid her head on the animal's neck. The horse bucked and trumpeted again, then sped off toward the hills, Nesrin's silk skirt blowing in the breeze like a colorful banner.

"Holy—" Parker had never seen such a stunt. Or known anyone to do something so stupid. Nesrin was going to get herself killed.

He lowered Amy to the ground.

"Rusty, you take care of the kids. Pete, Buck," he called to the hired hands standing around looking as dumbfounded as he was, "get some horses saddled.

We're going to have to go after that crazy female."
They'd probably find her with more broken bones than
good sense.

"Don't look like that'll be necessary, boss," Rusty
drawled, scratching at the back of his nearly bald head.
"That there little lady's bringing ol' Lucifer back on her
own."

Incredibly, Nesrin had turned the horse and was
trotting back toward the barn, her arms still wrapped
around the animal's neck. From where Parker stood, it
looked as if she were whispering in the horse's ear.

"Get the corral gate open," Parker told one of his
men. "Looks to me like Nesrin's a better hand than you
three are when it comes to catching mustangs."

Pete grinned back at him, showing a wide gap between his front teeth. "She's that 'n' more," he agreed.

Lucifer got skittery as he approached the corral gate,
but Nesrin's soft words and the lure of his mares did the
trick. She hustled him inside, slid off the horse and
scurried out the gate as the hired hands swung it closed
behind her. She beamed up at Parker.

"Where'd you learn to ride like that?" he asked in
admiration.

"It is nothing, master. Besides being a magician, my
father raised the finest horses in all of Persia. He taught
me to ride before I could walk."

Persia? he thought in a quick double take. That
hadn't been the country's name in years. "You could
have gotten yourself killed."

"Oh, no, the horse would not have harmed me. I only needed to tell him how brave and courageous he was to try to rescue his mares."

Tell him in what language? Parker wondered. She'd been something else on that horse—a mythical enchantress who could tame the wildest beast. His blood was still pumping adrenalin and he wanted to yank her into his arms and—

"You may have just saved my bacon," he said instead of acting on his impulse.

Her eyes widened. "You would turn that magnificent animal into *bacon?*"

"No, no. I meant the stallion's probably worth half again as much as all the mares combined. And right now I could use the extra cash."

A relieved "oh" escaped her lips.

"Wow!" Kevin interjected, gazing up at Nesrin with awestruck admiration. "I never saw *anybody* ride a horse like that."

"Kevin," she whispered on a soft sigh Parker wished had been meant for him. Slowly she brushed her fingertips to the side of the boy's face. "Yes, so handsome, as your mother often said. And smart like your father, with your computers and your books. Is that not so?"

The boy blushed and shrugged. "Yeah, I guess," he mumbled.

"And you, my sweet little Amy." Smiling, Nesrin knelt before the child who had joined her brother. "As pretty as a picture, they said, and it is so. And look, you brought your dolly with you to this new place."

Amy nodded. "She 'n' me have been visitin' the kitties."

"And did she like them?"

"Uh-huh. She's gonna help me pick one for my very own. When they don't need their mommy anymore."

Parker lifted his hat and swiped his palm across his sweat-dampened hair. What was going on? he wondered. Nesrin didn't even seem winded by her wild ride and was now far more interested in meeting the kids. Children she was already supposed to know, *if* she'd been a part of Marge's household for years.

Nothing had seemed quite right since Nesrin had appeared out of the shipping crate. Parker felt very much out of sync and unsettled. That wasn't like him at all. He was the kind of guy who was used to being in control...everything by the book. That's what his father had insisted upon, and a lifetime of military schools had reinforced that same lesson many times over.

Somehow he had the uncomfortable feeling Nesrin's arrival had changed the rules.

"Uncle Parker, I'm hungry," Amy pleaded. "Can we eat dinner now?"

"Told ya you shoulda eaten on the plane," Kevin said.

Amy stuck out her tongue and made a gagging sound. "That stuff was barfy."

"Was not!"

"That's enough, kids!" Parker ordered. He checked the lengthening rays of the sun, deciding the kids' schedules were probably so mixed up they had no idea what meal was actually due. After all, they'd been more than twenty-four hours en route from the Middle East.

That didn't change the fact he felt ill equipped to accept the role of both mother and father for two youngsters he hardly knew. He hadn't experienced much in the way of love as a child. It seemed unlikely he'd have enough left over to share with his niece and nephew.

At the same time, he knew the last thing Marge would have wanted was to have their father—the General—raise her kids for her.

Parker slanted a glance at Nesrin. There was magic in her uncertain smile, a plea no man could refuse. Perhaps she *was* a genie capable of casting a spell—on him.

He didn't need another hired hand, he realized, good rider or not. What he needed was . . .

But he couldn't ask for that. The fact was, with the added responsibility of the kids, he had a more important priority and figured he ought to be damn grateful Nesrin had almost literally fallen into his lap.

"Do you know how to cook?" he inquired instead.

She beamed him a smile that would have melted a winter snowpack.

"Oh, yes. My mother taught me a long time ago. I can make sarma and shish kebab. Boiled sheep brains are my specialty, though. They're quite delicious mixed with dried dates."

"Gross," Kevin announced.

Parker mentally echoed the same sentiment, swallowing hard. "I'm sure they're wonderful." And he supposed he'd eaten worse, but he couldn't remember when. "How 'bout we forget immigration for the moment." He had a few high-level connections in the government. Maybe he could work out a green card for Nesrin, just to keep things legal.

"Come on, kids," he said as he slid his hand to the center of Nesrin's back—mostly to give himself an excuse to touch her, as though he needed to confirm she was real. He headed her toward the house. "I'll show you the kitchen and you can whip up whatever you'd like for supper. If you don't mind being a combination nanny, chief cook and bottle washer," he belatedly said, "maybe we can work out a deal."

"Yes, please. I would be happy to serve you in any way you wish."

That opened a whole range of possibilities that tweaked Parker's imagination, most of which he didn't dare consider in any specific detail, and certainly not in front of the kids. "Great." His throat closed around the word. "And maybe you can find some clothes in Marge's stuff that would be a little more, ah, suitable for you to wear around the ranch."

Her smooth forehead drew into a frown, and she looked down at her silken skirt as though puzzled by his request. "As you wish, master."

"Parker," he corrected as he escorted her up the steps to the wide porch that spread across the width of the old ranch house.

"Parker," she echoed in a voice so soft and sweet it reminded him of a summer creek rippling over a bed of granite rocks.

OH, CAMEL DROPPINGS! Nesrin silently complained. Never in her long life had she ever imagined a house like this. The cooking area Parker had led her to was as strange and unfamiliar as the men's side of a mosque. How would she ever prepare a meal for him in such a wondrous place filled with dozens of cupboards and shiny metal devices? She was used to an open fire, a few sticks of wood and some dung for fuel. Here, simply finding a flame seemed impossible.

She wanted to please this man named Parker. He was truly an impressive wizard, to have helped her escape from the lamp, and she would not want to anger him so that he would send her back into the dreadful darkness.

He was mightily handsome, too, she conceded, this first human she had seen in many years. His eyes were the color of a lush green oasis on a sunlit day, she recalled. Across the hard angles and planes of his face, the sun had cast fascinating shadows. And his strength . . . He had held her in his arms, against the rock hardness of his chest as effortlessly as a strong man lifts a child. In contrast, she'd felt an excitement that hadn't seemed at all childish.

No, she definitely did not want to displease this brave man who had risked his life to save sweet Amy when she had been threatened by the magnificent stallion.

If only she weren't quite so inept at casting spells.

She called the children to her. "Kevin. Amy. You must help me, for I fear I do not know how to prepare a meal to please your Uncle Parker."

"I want peanut butter," Amy whined.

"Come on, sis. You can't have peanut butter for dinner."

The child puffed out her lower lip. "Why not? Uncle Parker always sent us big boxes full at Christmas. He must like it, too."

"That's 'cause Mom couldn't buy any stuff like that in the village market."

Nesrin slanted Kevin a glance. "Is it true? Your uncle sent you this thing called peanut butter?"

"Yeah. I suppose."

"And how do you fix it?"

"It's easy. You just make a sandwich."

Something easy. That's what Nesrin needed for now. Later she would learn to prepare other meals that would please Parker as much.

"Would you show me, Kevin?"

"Sure." He shrugged. "It's cool."

Actually, Nesrin had felt strangely warm and flushed ever since Parker had held her in his arms, not cool. And the ride on Lucifer had not chilled her flesh in the least. But she did not believe it necessary to point out that incongruity to Kevin while the boy was helping her fix dinner.

Kevin's demonstration of sandwich-making was quite brief. He rather quickly lost interest in the task and both children wandered off to explore the rest of the house.

Nesrin hooked the back of her wrist on her hip. It was such a simple job to make this meal, she was sure she could conjure up just the right number of sandwiches for their supper without any trouble at all. She did have a sample, she rationalized. All she need do is make that one little sandwich multiply for four. A decided time-saver, she thought.

Closing her eyes, she concentrated as hard as she could—without using so much of her power as to damage the house, she hastily reminded herself. She took a deep breath and began a very simple incantation in her head.

When she looked, she groaned aloud. Her cursed powers had misbehaved again!

Chapter Two

"Hey, look, Uncle Parker," Kevin exclaimed as he shoved in through the swinging door into the kitchen, Amy tagging along right behind him. "Nesrin's made enough sandwiches for an army."

Parker followed the kids inside and came to a quick halt. Peanut butter sandwiches? Dozens of them piled in a two foot-high stack on a huge serving plate in the middle of the maple table?

He shook his head in disbelief. There were enough for several armies, he agreed.

His gaze slid around the empty counters, and he noted the absence of anything cooking on the stove. "That's it for dinner?" he asked. Not that he thought any of them would leave the table hungry. He simply hadn't been aware there were that many loaves of bread available in all of Colorado.

"Kevin said we should wait until you arrived before we poured the milk," Nesrin explained, anxiously twisting a bit of silk through her fingers. "That way it will stay cold in your magical white box until you are ready to eat.''

"Sounds reasonable to me," he conceded, eyeing the refrigerator. He'd never heard it described as magical. But then, he'd never known a woman who thought she'd been released from a lamp... or one who put together a hundred peanut butter sandwiches for a dinner for four. Quirky but cute.

A smile twitched at the corners of his lips. "Well, come on, guys. Chow time." He twirled a chair around and straddled it backward.

The kids scurried to take their places at the table, Kevin imitating Parker's action with the chair. When Nesrin finished pouring the milk, Parker nodded for her to join them. He figured peanut butter sandwiches beat boiled brains, even mixed with dates, any day of the week.

From lowered lids, Nesrin observed Parker as he selected a sandwich from the enormous pile she had conjured with her faulty spell. He was watching her, too, in a way that made her feel acutely female, although his expression gave away nothing of his thoughts. An intensely private man, she concluded, one who rarely found reason to smile.

From the crinkles at the corners of his eyes she knew he'd spent years squinting into the sun. His face and neck were burnished to a golden brown, his muscular forearms roughened by a light covering of hair. His blue work shirt tugged at his broad shoulders. She'd noted earlier the way his trousers hugged narrow hips above long, powerful legs.

A man to be reckoned with in any century, she mused. But one she must be wary of. At some deep, intuitive level she knew Parker Dunlap was the kind of man to whom she might submit with the least little encouragement. Such a foolish act would surely bring down Rasheyd's curse on her head once again, and she could not possibly endure a return to the darkness of the lamp. This time with no hope for escape. Forever.

"Hey, Uncle Parker, can I start learning to ride tomorrow?" Kevin asked.

"I don't see why not. If you're willing to do chores around the place as part of the deal, I'll ask Rusty to pick out a gentle mount for you. But you can't go riding off by yourself. Okay?"

"Yeah, I guess," Kevin agreed with a lack of enthusiasm.

"Me, too," Amy demanded.

Parker frowned. Every time he looked at Amy, a band of love and regret tightened around his chest. She was the image of Marge, and her presence made Parker's protective instinct raise its head in a way he hadn't experienced in a good many years. Or with anyone except his sister, for that matter. "I don't know. You're still a little young...."

Amy's chin puckered.

"Perhaps she could ride with me," Nesrin offered, sensing both sibling rivalry and a tired child's tantrum in the making if Amy didn't get her way.

"Not on Lucifer," Parker warned.

"Of course not. I will be most careful with Amy. Your friend Rusty will choose a suitable horse for us, I am sure."

Realizing his gruff response had very nearly generated a fountain of tears on Amy's part, Parker added, "Maybe after I get the mustangs sold, and if there's any money left over, we could find you a pony to ride. That'd be more your size."

"Really, Uncle Parker?" Amy beamed him a smile. "I'm gonna get my very own horse?"

"A pony... in a few weeks. *If* I can find a good one for you."

To Nesrin's great relief, Parker seemed to have avoided a minor crisis with Amy. She thought he was a good man but very stern with the children. She would have to help him gentle his ways.

"Kevin found some bees," Amy announced, her mouth full of peanut butter. "He almost got stung."

"Tattler!" Kevin accused.

Parker raised his eyebrows. "What bees?"

"Aw, just some ol' bees around the back of the barn." The boy shrugged. "They didn't get me, or anything."

Parker thought he knew what the boy was talking about and didn't like the idea of Kevin fooling around the nest. "Those are mud wasps, son, and I don't want you to mess with them. I'll get Rusty and the boys to knock down the nest first thing in the morning."

"I'm sure Kevin would not do anything foolish," Nesrin said, giving the boy a fleeting smile of encouragement.

Parker wasn't so sure. He'd been about nine the year he shot a homemade arrow right through the open window of a laundry truck. It had been a wonder the darn thing had flown at all, much less straight, but that hadn't lessened the driver's anger. Or his father's fury.

He figured he'd better keep a close eye on Kevin.

As Parker took a second sandwich from the stack, he wondered how a delicate woman like Nesrin, almost fragile looking, could bring such change to the kitchen. The stainless appliances no longer seemed harsh in the bright light, but somehow softer; the stark white of the walls now reflected the warm pastels of her skirt. Nesrin was a provocation that was both soothing and disturbing at the same time. It made him think about things he'd missed—family, a loving woman, assorted other fantasies that were only a figment of a songwriter's imagination.

In an objective sense, he supposed she wasn't beautiful. Vibrant came to mind—a small, sexy package filled with dynamite.

Her mouth was mobile, smiling easily as she carried on a running conversation with Amy about her doll and Kevin on the subject of horses. Her nose and cheekbones were classic, like an artist might sculpt—or a man would want to rain kisses on. In spite of her small size, her legs were strong, like a dancer's, and he could easily imagine them wrapped powerfully around his waist.

He'd felt instant attraction for a few women in the past. Even for a guy who prided himself on self-control, it happened. But nothing like this. The feeling was hot, flowing through his veins in a thermal current.

Regret slid through him like a cold shower. He wasn't going to act on his baser instincts. He wasn't going to take advantage of a woman who thought she was a genie—or lied compulsively to get what she wanted. His sister, Marge, was the one who picked up strays. Not Parker.

But he wasn't so noble that he would turn her in to immigration for illegal entry. It had been obvious all during dinner that the kids needed a woman around, someone sympathetic who knew a lot more about raising children than he did. He'd just have to learn to keep his hands to himself and a handle on his thoughts.

THE CHILDREN HAD GONE to bed and the house was quiet as Nesrin stood in the front yard, enjoying the warm velvet of a summer night caressing her cheeks. She tilted her head back. Frogs and crickets called from the trees and grasses that surrounded Parker's house, setting up a chorus that masked the sounds of the restless horses in the corral. The air was tangy with the scent of pine and low-growing sage. After all the lonely years, she was finally in an oasis of tranquillity beneath a sky filled with stars.

She had all but forgotten how bright the dome of a night sky could be. No fear here of eternal darkness, only the wonder of the movement of the planets above the earth, and the quest for what those movements might foretell for her future.

Behind her she heard the squeak of the screen door and booted footsteps on the porch.

Parker. The name trembled through her awareness like a shimmering star.

He didn't speak, though she knew he stood not far from her. His silence settled as warmly around her as the sweet-smelling air and she caught his musky aroma, leather and something very male. She absorbed his essence through her pores along with the vast grandeur of the land. Without knowing it, this was a place she had always wanted to be.

"You were good with the kids tonight." His voice was low and oddly rough, so intimate it did not disturb the night.

"Even when weary from a long journey, they are easy children to love."

"For you, maybe. I'm not used to having kids around."

She turned at the sharp twist of bitterness in his words. "You have never married?"

"Yeah, I was married. She didn't want to ruin her figure by getting pregnant."

"That seems a strange thing for a woman to say." Even more troubling to learn Parker had a wife whom Nesrin had not seen. "Your wife...the women's quarters are somewhere nearby?"

"We're divorced."

"You set your wife aside?" she said, aghast at the cruelty of a man sending his wife away as though she were nothing more than an aging pack animal, easily discarded.

He laughed in a way that held no humor. "She married me thinking I'd be a general like my father and she'd have all the perks that went with the job. Some women thrive on having the wives of junior officers kowtowing to them. And I think Joyce pictured me as being Chief of Staff, dinners at the White House, that sort of thing. As soon as I shattered my ankle and had to resign from the army, she knew my career was over. So she called it quits for our marriage, too."

Nesrin could scarcely imagine a woman leaving a man like Parker. Certainly, among her people, she knew he would have been a leader. He moved with authority and had already demonstrated bravery when he had raced to save little Amy from the runaway horse. That he had been injured surprised her for she had detected no weakness at all.

"The gods must have wondered at her foolishness," Nesrin said, reproachful of the unseen woman.

She thought he smiled then, a slow curving of his mouth that crept up his face and stirred a fluttery warmth somewhere in her midsection, like the wings of invisible butterflies.

"I'll tell her you said so next time she asks for an increase in her alimony check."

She smiled back at him, though she doubted he could see her clearly. "You must not worry about the children. They already care for you. Kevin wants to please you so much he has begun to imitate how you walk and the way you sit at the table.''

''I don't know. To me, with that darn ponytail of his and the sloppy way he dresses, he looks like the kind of kid who'd never make it through boot camp. He's mischief on the way to happening.''

''He is only nine years old,'' she observed.

''I suppose.'' Parker lifted his hip to rest it on the split rail fence separating the yard from the rest of the ranch. Nesrin, he noted, had found a pair of Marge's jeans. They were a size or two too big and she'd used a silken scarf for a belt. She created a very appealing picture in the starlight, the silhouetted flair of her hips, the swell of her breasts in a T-shirt that fit a lot snugger than the jeans and her dark hair so long it hung to her waist.

Curious why she should have been so anxious to get to the States, he asked, ''Don't you have family back in your country who will be worried about you?''

''No, I do not think so,'' she said thoughtfully. ''In a way, it was my father who sent me away. After all these years, he would not be expecting my return.''

A peculiar response but he let it slide. ''No other family?''

''Two older brothers. Quite handsome and very clever. When I was young they watched over me much as Kevin cares for his sister. I think I caused them a great deal of trouble and embarrassment. They are well rid of me, I imagine.'' She shrugged nonchalantly but Parker wondered if she cared more than she let on.

"There's no husband?" he persisted.

"Oh, no. My father had not yet arranged a marriage for me. Perhaps because—" her voice caught "—I may not have been found acceptable by any man of my class."

An anger swift and fierce swept over Parker. He held himself back from pulling her into his arms, from telling her she was damn acceptable for any man who had eyes and she should never settle for an arranged marriage. It ought to be her choice.

Instead he said roughly, "Some guys are fools, too."

She turned away from him, leaning her hands on the rail fence, and gazed up into the sky, but he sensed she was pleased by what he had said. There'd been a time in his life when he'd have gone after a woman like Nesrin, quirky or not. He would have had her between his sheets before she knew what was happening. That no longer seemed fair. Over the years he'd begun to question what he really had to offer a woman. Sex was a fleeting thing and love seemed beyond his capacity. He'd certainly failed miserably with his ex, though he wasn't entirely sure he carried the whole blame for that fiasco.

He cleared his throat. "Ranching starts early around here. It's time we turned in."

"Yes. I'll go in soon. I want to enjoy the fresh air for a moment or two more."

Nesrin listened while Parker retreated up the steps to the porch and entered the house through the squeaky front door. She had wanted so much to hug him for what he'd said—for how he had understood her anguish that no man had wanted her as his bride. After all, an inept genie was hardly the kind of woman a man would select for his life's mate.

In contrast to the views of men of her village, Parker's words had given her so much pleasure she doubted her legs would have carried her the distance to the house without making a fool of herself in his presence.

Gathering herself, she took one last glance at the glorious sky, then went inside.

The room she'd been assigned contained a wide bed so soft she sank into the mattress as though it were a fluffy cloud. Gratefully she gazed up at the light that had no wick, that glowed softly beside the bed even as her eyelids grew heavy. She dropped off to sleep with the comforting knowledge that whenever she woke there would be light in her room, and that Parker was nearby. For the first time in a very long while, she felt doubly blessed.

PARKER JAMMED HIS PILLOW into a tight wad of stuffing and flopped over onto his stomach. He groaned.

How was a man supposed to sleep with a woman like Nesrin right down the hall? Ten steps to her door, he mentally calculated. Thirty feet, give or take a little. A few more strides and he'd be next to her bed.

And do what? he chided himself.

Less than twenty-four hours ago she'd appeared in the back of his pickup, and since then he'd imagined ravishing her about a dozen different times. So far.

Actually, it had been kind of a continuous exercise in self-control, with more moments of high-level arousal than not.

Dragging himself out of bed long before dawn, after a mostly sleepless night, he pulled on his jeans and work boots, and tugged on a shirt. Rolling up the sleeves to mid-forearm, he decided hard work was the best way to reduce his frustration. Lucifer ought to be a satisfactory distraction for a guy who didn't want to take a cold shower this early in the morning.

He had to admit, by capturing the wild stallion, Nesrin had probably saved the ranch for him. Suddenly it looked as if he'd soon be rid of the horrendous bank loan he'd taken out to pay off his ex-wife, and the bank wouldn't have a chance to sell this little bit of the Rockies to some uncaring conglomerate.

He'd still have his dream.

Parker entered the corral making soft reassuring sounds to calm the mares that were bunched in one corner of the ring. His lariat dangled comfortably from his hand.

With a proud lift of his head, Lucifer snorted a challenge. He stood protectively in front of his harem.

"Easy boy. We're just going to get acquainted for a while."

Lucifer wasn't interested in making friends. He pawed the ground and huffed his displeasure.

"Yeah, I know. You're a tough guy. But I've met tougher." The men who'd been under his command in Special Forces had been the same kind of uncompromising breed as Lucifer. Rugged, anxious to prove themselves and a little on the wild side. They didn't tame easily. Parker could respect that in a man or a horse.

He cut Lucifer away from his mares. "How'd you ever let that little wisp of a woman have her way with you yesterday? Better not let that news get around, buddy. It'll ruin your image."

With a sound that was equal parts grunt and groan, Parker realized Nesrin had accomplished what no woman had since he'd been sixteen and filled with raging hormones—half a lifetime ago. No matter what he did, he couldn't seem to keep his mind off her.

Parker worked with Lucifer, letting his lariat slide off the stallion's rump, getting the animal used to his scent, until the pink promise of dawn lifted golden above the hills surrounding the valley. Usually by now his hired hands had put in an appearance.

Frowning, Parker ended Lucifer's first lesson and went in search of them. As he headed for the back door, he noticed Kevin going out the front.

"Hey, Kevin, what's up?"

He shrugged. "Nothin'."

"You'll stay out of trouble, won't you?"

"Sure. I'm just looking around."

Parker figured he couldn't keep an eye on the boy twenty-four hours a day, and get his work done, so he let Kevin go, hoping he'd use common sense around the ranch. He supposed he was a bit edgy about the kid.

After all, at that age Parker had been a magnet for trouble.

As he shoved through the back door, he realized Rusty, Pete and Buck were in the kitchen. As a rule they never came to the main house for breakfast. They ate in the bunkhouse, insisting they preferred to fix their own meals.

Now Parker discovered them crowding around in the kitchen looking like a bunch of aging hound dogs sniffing around a bitch in heat. Parker wondered why that made him so damn mad. It wasn't as if he had any special agreement with Nesrin. She was, after all, an employee of sorts, free to talk to any man she darn well pleased. He simply wished she didn't appear so thoroughly engrossed in the inane conversation.

Unnoticed, Parker folded his arms across his chest and leaned against the doorjamb. Either Nesrin was leading his hired hands around by the nose with her quick smile and the cute little shimmy of her behind, or she had lived in the remotest village in all of the Mid-East. Which couldn't be the case since she claimed she'd been part of Marge's household. Parker knew darn well Marge hadn't lived in a mud hut, but in a presentable house in a fair-size village.

"This here is how you get the water, ma'am," Rusty said. He lifted the handle of the faucet and water splashed into the sink.

Startled, Nesrin jumped back. She was wearing a blue sundress tied at the waist with a silk scarf. Her quick movement started the skirt swaying, the hem brushing right at the curve of her calf, which Parker's hand ached to palm. One dress strap slipped off her slender shoulder and unselfconsciously she lifted it back into place in a gesture another woman might have meant as a tease. Parker didn't know what Nesrin had on her mind, but it sure as hell was grating on his imagination. He was glad the day hadn't heated up yet, because he was already sweating.

Laughing in her clear, crystalline way, she said, "You mean I do not have to haul water from a well?"

"No, ma'am." Rusty slid the coffeepot under the spigot. "We got ourselves a well, all right, but this here way is a whole bunch easier."

"Oh, yes, I can see that." She bestowed a brilliant smile on the aging cowhand.

Rusty continued explaining the fine art of coffee-making, then Pete took over to demonstrate the workings of an electric stove. Buck looked set to take on the dishwasher as his lesson in modern kitchen management when Parker called a halt to the classroom activities.

"Seems to me we have a ranch to run, gentlemen," he said, moving into the room the way an officer converges on enlisted men who have been negligent of their duty. "And a dozen mustangs to break. If we leave the lady to her own devices, I'm sure she'll get along just fine."

"Yes, boss," they said in unison. The over-the-hill gang was far too old to have been caught ogling a woman. At least they had the good sense to look sheepish as they edged out the back door. Or maybe they were simply taking their time as they got one last good look at Nesrin.

"Your friends are very nice," she said once the others had left. It was clear Parker was not pleased with her. His scowl deepened the lines across his forehead and narrowed his oasis green eyes. He seemed tightly coiled in his anger, like a desert falcon just before he dives toward his prey. She wished she could conjure up a magical spell that would make him smile.

In her mind's eye she imagined a grin of delight creasing his cheeks and even heard him laugh, a rough raspy sound as though his sense of humor had grown rusty with disuse. The vision seemed so real it sent a wave of pleasure through her.

Then she blinked and the image was gone.

Parker cleared his throat and rubbed his palm over his face, as if he'd been aware of her vision, too. But, of course, Nesrin wasn't capable of casting a spell that would make this man truly smile. At least she thought such a clever deed was beyond her powers.

"Rusty and the boys kind of came with the place when I bought it a couple of years ago," he said hesitantly, shaking his head as though coming back from some sort of a reverie. "I'm lucky to get a half day's work out of them between games of checkers and afternoon naps on the front porch of the bunkhouse."

"And still you do not send them away?" she asked in surprise.

He shrugged, his fingertips jammed into his back pockets. "I'd fire them, but I don't think they have anywhere else to go."

As gruff as Parker might sometimes seem, Nesrin noted he was also kind. Among her people, an older worker was dismissed with little thought to what might become of him—even if it meant beggary, or worse, starvation. Perhaps Parker did not even recognize the generous spirit that dwelt within him.

"Did you wish me to prepare your morning meal?" she asked, feeling a sense of admiration for Parker sweep through her, which she firmly tried to squelch. She dared not allow herself to become too attracted to a man who might be her downfall.

"How are you with pancakes?"

She searched her memory. She had heard the word spoken in his sister's household, but did not know the ingredients or the method of cooking such a dish. If only she had been able to peer out through the lamp she would have been far better prepared for her release into a modern world.

From outside the house came the sound of a ruckus and a good deal of shouting. A horse whinnied in alarm.

"Get away from them dern things!"

"You're riling the horses!"

"You're a-gonna git yourself stung, boy!"

"Help!" a child wailed.

Nesrin met Parker's eyes for a brief instant before realization struck home.

"Kevin!" they cried in unison, and raced toward the door.

Chapter Three

At the center of the swarm of wasps, Kevin gamely tried to escape, first by swatting at them, then by turning on his heel and running away as fast as he could. Like the tail of a comet, the wasps followed him.

"Uncle Parker!" he wailed.

"I'm coming, son."

With a frenzied whinny, Lucifer reared and clubbed the corral fence with his forelegs, making a concerted effort to release himself and his mares from the trap of the enclosure.

Parker tossed his shirt over Kevin to give the boy some protection from the wasps, leaving his own back bare, a ready target for the crazed insects.

Panic and fear clawed at Nesrin. Without giving any thought to her inconsistent abilities to cast spells, she closed her eyes and wished the wasps away with all of her might.

"I'll be derned!" Rusty shouted. "Where'd all them birds come from?"

Birds?

Nesrin opened her eyes. Black birds filled the sky. Big, *hungry* black birds. Hundreds of them. They swooped in on the horde of wasps like Mongol invaders attacking remote villages through secret mountain passes. The wasps scattered. Some were gobbled up in the air, while others were knocked to the ground where the birds turned them into a more leisurely snack.

The air reverberated with the sound of flapping wings and the caw of birds.

Within minutes, it was all over. There weren't any more wasps in sight and the birds had taken flight, streaming in a dark ribbon against the blue sky as they arrowed toward the distant mountain peaks.

Exhaling in relief, Nesrin smiled a secret smile. It wasn't exactly the spell she'd hoped to cast, but the birds had certainly proved a successful strategy to protect Kevin and Parker. She would have to remember later just how she had accomplished such a feat.

She almost laughed aloud at the stunned expressions on the faces of Parker and his friends. Perhaps there was some hope for her yet as a worthwhile genie.

Amy came running out from the safety of the house as Parker asked, "Is everybody all right?" His hand rested protectively on Kevin's shoulder.

"They got me, Uncle Parker. Real bad."

"Yeah, I know, kid." He glanced toward the corral. "We're just darn lucky Lucifer and his mares didn't escape. That would have made your crazy stunt pretty darn expensive." It might have cost both the ranch and Parker's guardianship of the kids. The financial edge he'd been treading led to a precipitous drop with a single misstep.

Kevin bent his head in apology.

"Tell me, boy, when you were with your folks, did you get into trouble a lot?"

Looking sheepish, he said, "Mom called me the best trouble finder she'd ever met—except for you, Uncle Parker."

He quirked his lips into a knowing smile. "Guess it's genetic then 'cause your mom would have known." He squeezed the boy's shoulder. "Come on. Let's get those stings taken care of."

"YOU HAVE BEEN VERY BRAVE not to cry," Nesrin told Kevin as she daubed ointment on the stings that covered his back. His chin had wobbled any number of times, but still she wanted him to feel courageous.

"Those darn wasps sure got mad," he said. Looking glum, he was sitting on the closed toilet seat in the upstairs bathroom.

"Perhaps you would be angry, too, if someone was knocking down your house with a stick."

"I suppose." He frowned and scratched at one of the welts. "How come all those birds showed up at once? That was really weird."

"It is fortunate that such magical things can happen."

He looked skeptical. "Magic?"

With her fingertips, she combed back his blond hair and placed a soft kiss on his forehead. She wished all of her spells would result in such clever solutions to nettlesome problems. "Go play quietly for a time so the ointment can do its work."

From his place in the bathroom doorway where he'd been watching the doctoring process, Parker said, "And see if you can stay out of trouble for a while."

"Can I use your computer?" Kevin asked.

Parker raised his eyebrows. "You know about computers?"

"Sure. My dad let me mess with his all the time. We were hooked up to a net that had math games and stuff. It was cool."

"Yeah? Well, okay, but don't dump the hard disk. That's got all my records on it."

"I won't." With a confident smile, Kevin slipped out the door and hurried from sight.

"Thanks for playing nursemaid," Parker said, turning to Nesrin.

"I am pleased to be of help."

"I'd appreciate it though if you'd lay off with the magic business. I don't want the kid confused."

Her shoulders fell with dejection. Even if her spells weren't all they should be, the magic was real. She wished she could tell Parker she'd been the one to conjure up the flock of birds that had saved both him and the boy from additional stings. But, of course, he wouldn't believe her.

"As you wish," she agreed, gesturing toward the seat Kevin had vacated. "Your turn now for the medicine."

"I'm okay."

"The stingers must be pulled and poison must be drawn by the ointment, or you may become ill."

"They only got me in a couple of places. No big deal."

She eyed him thoughtfully. "Is it possible a grown man has not as much bravery as a young boy and so refuses the medicine?"

Her comment slammed right into the middle of Parker's ego. It wasn't a little medicine he was worried about. Or a few bothersome stings. Pure and simple, it was Nesrin who had him gritting his teeth against a different kind of pain.

All the time she'd been putting the lotion on Kevin's back, Parker had been watching her hands. Her slender fingers had moved with gentle ease over the boy's shoulders and back, reminding him of rose petals drifting in a breeze. Or the softness of a spring rain misting the landscape. He wasn't sure he could handle her touching him in the same way, yet he knew that was exactly what he wanted—and more.

He wanted, he realized with some alarm, to sweep her off her feet with romance—to take her dancing and see candlelight reflected in her dark eyes. He wanted to ply her with flowers and jewels, seduce her. If he could, he'd even write poems that praised her soft lips and the sweet lyrical sound of her voice.

But he couldn't do any of that. He felt a fraud even thinking such nonsense. He was in no position to romance any woman.

Figuring he was either a damn fool or a glutton for punishment, he shrugged out of his shirt and sat down on the closed lid of the stool, turning sideways so she could get to the welts on his back. As she moved closer he caught her scent—a subtle fragrance that a breeze would waft for miles over a dry desert to lure a traveler onward. A fascinating combination of heat and sweetness.

Nesrin hesitated, feeling alternately hot and cold. She had never seen a partially clothed man before—certainly not one so close. Among her people, the men had always been robed in her presence, even her brothers.

In spite of herself, she was fascinated by the breadth of Parker's shoulders, the splendid differences in texture between his masculine flesh and her softer skin. As her fingers mapped the contours of his back, muscles rippled in exciting waves, setting up a matching response deep inside her.

"Nesrin, what are you doing?"

Nervousness, and an emotion she couldn't quite identify, parched her throat. "You have several stings on your back."

"Yeah, well . . . let's get on with it."

Working more quickly, she dabbed the salve on each ugly welt. How unfortunate the angry wasps had marred such masculine perfection.

"You should try not to be upset with Kevin," she said. Nor should she be quite so aware of how the bright overhead light shone on Parker's hair, revealing a hundred different shades of gold and tawny brown among the strands. Earlier she had thought his hair a single sandy color, but she found the reality far more varied and exciting. "The boy did not mean to do harm."

"We're just lucky the horses didn't spook any worse than they did. If Lucifer had broken through the fence, we would have lost all the mares."

"I know he regrets his impulsiveness." As she must resist her desire to touch her lips to the fine speckles of darker color scattered across Parker's fair shoulders. Even that knowledge did not stop her from wondering how each small blemish might taste.

She glanced up and was speared by Parker's reflected gaze in the mirror. Something passed between them, as sharp as a sword but far more heated. It made her breath lock in her lungs. In an instant, she recalled rich green emeralds inlaid in elephant tusks, prized possessions of the wizard Rasheyd. They were there now in Parker's eyes, sparking with a different kind of danger.

"Enough!" He rose to his feet as if she had cut him.

"But there are more—"

"It doesn't matter."

"The welt on your neck is quite swollen."

"I'll take care of it myself." He snatched the tube of salve from her hand and dabbed some on his neck. His throat moved like that of an agitated camel.

"If I hurt you—"

"It's okay, Nesrin. Leave it be." Abruptly he tossed the tube of medicine onto the counter, whirled around and marched out the door.

"You still have not had your morning meal," she called after him.

"Forget it. I'm not hungry."

By midafternoon, Nesrin had still not discerned why Parker had seemed so upset with her. Nor had he come to the kitchen to eat any meal, which troubled her greatly. He worked hard and needed nourishment to see him through the day.

At the sound of a quick rap on the back door, Nesrin turned.

"Howdy. Kin I come in?" asked the woman who had shoved open the door. She was tall and angular, with graying hair and a smile that was all teeth. "I reckon the boys were right. You're about the purtiest little thing I've seen in a month of Sundays."

The heat of a blush swept up Nesrin's cheeks.

"Now don't you go gettin' flustered, honey. I came ridin' by, and Rusty and the fellas told me all about you." She extended her hand. Her grip was as strong as any man's and her palm just as rough.

"I'm Parker's closest neighbor. Louanne Wagner's my name. My spread's right over the next hill, not more 'n a couple miles from here." She paused long enough to catch her breath and glance around the kitchen. "Surely is nice to have a woman in the neighborhood again. I miss having a chance for some girl talk now and then. Figured, you being new 'n' all, you could use a friend, too."

An irrepressible smile climbed Nesrin's face. "I have not had a friend in a very long time."

"Well, you got one now, honey."

Nesrin had a thousand questions she wanted to ask and only another woman—a friend—would have the answers. But first she would ask Louanne to teach her how to prepare meals that would please Parker. Perhaps she could find some favor to offer in return.

THANK HEAVEN HIS LIBIDO was back under control.

After spending several hours breaking mustangs, Parker decided it was safe to go back into the house. Every bone in his body felt as though it had been dislocated by the jarring of his butt against the saddle—and sometimes against the ground. He figured he wouldn't even notice if ten thousand dancing girls went traipsing by.

He opened the front door, stepped into the living room and realized he'd figured dead wrong.

The eerie sound of wailing flutes and fluttering castanets thrummed from the stereo in lyrical quarter tones like music out of the *Arabian Nights*. Nesrin gyrated in rhythm to the quivering beat, dressed once again in the nearly transparent skirt she'd worn when he first saw her and the abbreviated top that left her midriff bare. She rippled stomach muscles Parker didn't know existed; flexed them in a way that made him sweat.

Her arms moved effortlessly, beckoning to any helpless man who might happen to pass by.

Louanne danced right next to her, awkwardly trying to follow her movements, all bony arms and legs, a big grin on her face. After a quick glance at his neighbor,

Parker riveted his attention solely on Nesrin. She heated his blood like sun on asphalt; she stirred his imagination with vibrant expectations. If there had been a thousand other dancers in the room, all of them gorgeous Las Vegas show girls, he still would have had eyes only for Nesrin.

That revelation stunned Parker.

This woman, who had mysteriously appeared in his life, had indeed cast some sort of a spell on him.

"Howdy, Parker. Whata ya think?" Louanne gave an extra rotation with her hips.

Parker stifled a smile. "I think you're either going to need a chiropractor, or you'll land husband number four if you carry on like that in public. Assuming you don't get arrested first."

"Hot diggity! I got my eye on this fella down at the feed store.... 'Course, he don't seem real interested. Guess I'll have to keep my eyes open for somebody else comin' down the pike." The music stopped and Louanne came to a halt, breathing hard. "Lord, this ol' body don't work like it used to."

Parker decided Nesrin's body was a piece of art, precision made to draw a man's eye and haunt his dreams. She was watching him warily, as though silently waiting for his approval. He wanted to applaud. Hell, he wanted to toss her over his shoulder, climb the stairs to his bedroom, and... But he wasn't going to do any of that—not if he wanted to keep his sanity.

"You two want to tell me what's brought on this dancing business?" he asked.

"This sweet little lady of yours," Louanne said, "has agreed to trade me a few dancin' lessons for some hints 'bout cookin'. Figured I couldn't pass up a deal like that."

For the first time, Parker caught a whiff from the kitchen—something rich and spicy and undoubtedly delicious.

"We're gonna work our way through chicken, beef and pork," Louanne continued. "Started her off with that enchilada casserole you had at my place a couple of months ago."

"Not sheep brains?" Parker questioned.

The older woman frowned, and he waved off her confusion at his wry remark.

"I hope you do not mind," Nesrin said, her voice as soft as the silken skirt she wore. "I only wished to please you, Parker."

Everything about Nesrin pleased him, and he could imagine she knew other ways to satisfy him beyond a dance or two—or one of Louanne's casseroles. Simply the way she pressed her lips together to say his name gave him a jolt of pure sexual fantasy.

"You can run the kitchen any way you want, Nesrin," he said. "I've got to... to take a shower." A cold one, he realized as he headed up the stairs. Or maybe he needed to reactivate the old icehouse out in back, though he doubted even that would cool down his libido below the boiling point as long as Nesrin was in his house.

Nesrin frowned, troubled by Parker's abrupt departure. She had hoped he might like her dancing.

"Well now, looks to me like that young fella has got himself a bee up his arse."

"He was stung *there?*" Nesrin asked incredulously.

"No, I don't mean that, sweetie." Louanne's laugh was rough and full-bodied. "I mean he's got a hankerin' for you. But then, any red-blooded man who was still breathin' would take an interest in a sweet little package like you. You're some kinda pretty, you are."

Nesrin was quite sure she didn't want Parker to "hanker" for her. That might lead to him wanting her to submit. And that would lead to her downfall because she wasn't at all confident she could resist. She got the oddest feelings when he looked at her, his eyes growing dark with a strange hunger. It was as though he had the power to drain her will.

She mustn't let that happen. From inside the lamp she had heard angry voices the day before she arrived at Parker's ranch. Though the words were muffled, she felt sure someone was upset the lamp had been packed in the crate. If that someone was Rasheyd...

Fear gripped her insides, and she turned pleading eyes toward Louanne. "What must I do so that Parker won't hanker for me?"

"Why, honey, every woman in the county would like to be able to spark that boy's interest. Not a one of 'em have caught his eye in the couple of years he's been here. Now you're tellin' me *you're* the one who's not interested?"

"It would be very dangerous for me. There is a man..."

"Your husband?"

"Oh, no, I would never wish to be Rasheyd's wife. He wanted me only for his harem."

Louanne snorted a disgusted sound. "Shucks, around here we only allow a fella to have one lady at a time, leastwise legally. I don't reckon you've got anything to worry about. I figure Parker would run off any *hombre* who came around sniffing after you."

Nesrin had not considered that possibility. Parker had seemed very protective of the children. Perhaps he would also protect her. Certainly he was a powerful wizard himself, although he might not recognize his own potency. He might well be a match for Rasheyd.

PARKER REINED his personal mount, Magnum, back toward the main ranch. The stallion responded to his light touch, eager to compete for the attention of the mares that had recently taken up residence in his territory. Parker tried not to consider that he was fighting the same kind of urge.

By gritting his teeth—and certain other parts of his anatomy—Parker had managed to get through a whole week since Nesrin's arrival. Things were getting easier, he told himself. Certainly the daily visits from Louanne meant meals were getting better, even if the sound of exotic music drifting out of the house every afternoon had other than a calming effect on him. The beat plucked too close to the bone to be relaxing; images of

Nesrin dancing struck too many erotic chords to allow him to forget the sight of her gyrating seductively in the middle of his living room.

When he wasn't breaking horses, Parker found himself heading for the far corners of his small empire in order to avoid confronting his own weakness. A single lithe woman shouldn't have such an all-consuming hold on his imagination. It showed a serious lack of concentration on his part, a shortcoming he had every intention of overcoming.

Other, odd things had been happening, too, since Nesrin and the kids had shown up.

One evening he'd followed the excited sound of Amy's giggles upstairs to her bedroom. It had looked to Parker as if the child were floating three feet above the bed on a billowing sheet. Just hanging there as though on top of a cloud. Very peculiar. Downright unbelievable.

"Look, Uncle Parker," Amy had cried. "A magic sheet just like a magic carpet!"

Nesrin, who was in the room, gasped, "Oh, my..." And Amy had plopped back onto the bed with a happy squeal.

Of course, Parker had assumed they'd only been playing and Amy had been bouncing on the bed. What he'd seen had been the fluttering of a sheet, a child playing. Nothing unusual about that.

But then, another time, he'd walked into the kitchen only to be met by a dozen place settings of silverware flying in formation toward the dinner table and a harassed Nesrin trying to snag them back again. He'd simply turned around and gone outside again, deciding he'd been working too hard. Hallucinations could happen to anyone, he assured himself.

Giving his head another shake, Parker tapped his heels to Magnum's sides and hurried the horse back to the corral. Having Nesrin around was a thoroughly unsettling experience.

Maybe Parker's general edginess accounted for his anxiety when he spotted Kevin poised in the open loft doors of the barn. It didn't take a genius to know the kid was about to play either Superman or the Lone Ranger. Given the poor old mare Amy held by the reins beneath the doors, Parker guessed the latter.

Dismounting, he shouted a warning. "Kevin!" But it was already too late.

The boy launched himself from his perch above the hapless horse. He missed his target by inches, frightening the animal as he bounced against the saddle then tumbled to the ground. Screaming, the mare reared and yanked herself free from Amy's grasp, hooves clawing the air.

"Kevin!" Amy cried out in alarm as she retreated from the horse.

Adrenaline drove Parker forward like a sprinter. Leaping over the corral fence as if it were half the height, he snatched Amy from the path of flying hooves at the same time he shouldered the mare out of the way, protecting Kevin's fallen form in the process. God,

Marge would never forgive him if he let anything happen to her kids.

In the excitement, Lucifer found his own surge of power and bolted over the top of the fence, forgetting his mares as he escaped toward the hills.

Parker's gut told him with a wrench that if the mares had followed the stallion, it would have meant the whole future of the ranch.

In the resulting chaos, kids cried, horses bellowed, the hired hands tried to calm the agitated mares, and Parker swore like a graduate of the streets, not the military academy. Only the soft hand that closed over his shoulder brought him back to reality.

"Are the children all right?" Nesrin asked.

Parker checked both youngsters. Outside of looking pale, they appeared to be whole. No blood. No obvious broken bones. "Yeah, I think so," he said. His breathing was coming hard and his heart beat like a sledgehammer against his ribs. He was mad at Kevin, and furious with himself. That damn stallion had been his best guarantee to keep the bank off his back.

"Then there is no great harm done." Nesrin's calm influence prevented Parker from throttling Kevin. Or hugging him because he'd been so scared for the boy's safety.

"No great harm? It was a stupid stunt," Parker insisted. "You could have gotten yourself killed, Kevin. Or Amy hurt. You put her in danger, too, you know."

"I'm sorry," Kevin muttered. Dirt streaked the boy's sweaty face and the kid's chin quivered.

"He almost made it," Amy said in sisterly defense. "The horse moved. It wasn't Kevin's fault."

Yeah, right. Parker figured he needed to put a leash on Kevin. The kid was nothing but trouble.

Just like he'd been, a silent voice of conscience reminded him, sounding a whole lot like his sister speaking.

In a velvet whisper of caring, Nesrin said, "Your nephew is a very brave young man. He has been practicing his riding all week and hoped to show you how much he had learned, but you have been away so much he has not had the chance. Perhaps tomorrow we can all go on a picnic together so he can show off his new skills."

"*Picnic?*" Parker echoed. If Parker's father had been in charge, the kid would have been rewarded for his reckless behavior with a verbal thrashing—not a picnic. At the very least he would have been ordered to march off about ten thousand demerits, West Point style—rain or shine.

"The boy seeks the special attention of a good man," she said. Her innocent doe eyes accused him of dereliction of duty.

He cursed under his breath. She was probably right. He'd been so set on avoiding Nesrin, and trying to get the mares saddle-broken, he'd ignored the fact that Kevin and Amy still needed his attention. It was damn tough for them to lose their parents and then to be thrown into a totally unfamiliar situation with an uncle they hardly knew.

Guilt lashed his conscience and he vowed to do better.

"Okay, you've got it. A picnic. Tomorrow." As his gaze shifted from Nesrin back to the kids, he wondered if he'd just made a poor decision. Kevin didn't look like the kind of youngster who would be satisfied with creating anything less than total bedlam. And hanging around with Nesrin was going to put a serious strain on Parker's already overworked libido.

The truth was, he shouldn't allow himself a single day off until the bank loan was paid. Making an effort to recapture Lucifer would make more sense than a picnic. Money in the bank meant a lot right now. But he'd already agreed....

"Come in," Parker responded to the knock on his office door.

Nesrin juggled a tray with mugs and a teapot as she entered. Hands full, she had to levitate the tray for an instant. It was really a simple little spell, but things got out of hand. As usual, she thought grimly. The mugs and pot drifted toward the ceiling. She scrambled to snatch them back, placing them carefully on the tray again.

Head bent, Parker was sitting behind a large desk stacked high with papers. A single desk lamp illuminated the room and an open window brought in the warm evening scent of the mountains.

Parker glanced up from his work. "Is something wrong?"

"No, no. You seemed so troubled at dinner," she said, catching her breath. "I thought you might wish a cup of tea to soothe you."

He leaned back in his leather chair and the springs protested. "I'm not sure tea will do the trick, but thanks for the thought."

"I am sorry Lucifer escaped." She set the mug on a spot he cleared of papers. "Perhaps he will return to visit his mares and we can capture him again."

"Maybe." He nodded his thanks for the tea, though that wasn't usually his beverage of choice. "Things are a little tight financially right now. The stallion would have made life easier but I think we'll get by. Just."

"You are a wise man and will find a way."

He hoped she was right. The stakes were higher than he liked. "I've got a contract to deliver twenty saddle-broken horses by the end of the month. If that happens, I'm home free. I'll pay off a loan I've got on the ranch and—"

"You are in debt to a moneylender?" She looked shocked.

With a shrug, he picked up an envelope from his desk and fingered it thoughtfully. The return address carried a familiar military emblem. "Assuming I can pay off the loan there'll be no way my father can get his hands on Kevin and Amy."

Nesrin sank slowly into the chair opposite Parker, her dark eyes filled with questions. "Your father wishes to take the children away from you?"

"That's what he says." He flicked the envelope with his fingernail. "He's about to retire from the army. Claims it's a perfect time for him to take over raising the kids."

"And you do not wish him to do that?"

A muscle rippled at his jaw. "I'll do anything short of murder to prevent it."

"But how could he do that? Surely, if your sister wished—"

"Marge didn't leave any last wishes. At least not in writing. But we'd talked about it once, after Kevin was born. She made me promise I'd take care of her kids if anything happened to her and Jack."

"Then you must keep your promise."

"I plan to." He shifted the envelope in his hands, knowing he'd have to fight his father in court, if it came to that. "My dad has this idea that he's a great parent. Unfortunately, he's got a fair number of connections in the private sector and wouldn't be beneath using them to get his way. The *right* way, he'd say. If I lose the ranch, and it looked like I couldn't provide a decent home for the kids, then a judge might believe him."

"We will simply tell the judge the truth. The children love you." Nesrin lifted her chin at a stubborn angle.

Parker smiled tiredly. He hoped it would be as easy as Nesrin suggested. Better yet, he hoped he could convince his father not to challenge the existing guardianship arrangement. And that meant he couldn't risk losing the ranch.

As Nesrin sipped her tea, she imagined in her mind's eye Parker as the powerful leader she knew he should be. A sultan, she thought, ruler of a desert tribe, his turban decorated with a huge ruby, his fingers weighted with precious jewels. He would hold court in his lavish throne room, his subjects bowing to his will.

Yes, she could even see his father humbling himself on his knees before the mighty Parker.

"Your wish is my command," the old man would say, his voice trembling with fear as the wind blew warm through the doorway.

"You will leave the children in my care," Parker would insist.

"Yes. Oh mighty sultan. It shall be as you desire."

Nesrin smiled. If only she had the power to make such a scene come true.

"Does it seem awfully hot in here?" Parker asked. He wiped his hand across his forehead.

Blinking herself back from images of her homeland, she said, "No, I do not think so."

"It's just that I thought...there for a minute..." He shrugged. "It was like there was a hot desert wind blowing through the window. I must really be worried about the kids and my father. I'm half losing my mind."

Nesrin swallowed a giggle. She had not known she could conjure images others could feel. "I am sure all will be well." Though with her erratic powers, she must use great care in the spells she cast. It would not do to accidentally transport Parker to some unknown land.

Chapter Four

"You are it, Kevin," Nesrin sang out.

She played tag with the children, darting between boulders and through a stand of aspen, dodging this way and that to elude them. She dashed around the tethered horses they'd ridden up into the hills—Parker's powerful stallion Magnum and the two mares she and Kevin had ridden, Amy safely tucked in front of her on the saddle. Fortunately, they had convinced Amy to leave her beloved calico cat Sushan at the ranch.

Lighthearted, Nesrin's laughter carried her song of joy above the murmuring water flowing swiftly over granite rocks in a nearby creek. Above her, silver green leaves shimmered in an unseen breeze. She cherished the freedom to run, to feel the sun on her face and the uneven surface of the earth beneath her sandaled feet.

So many years had been wasted; too many moments spent in lonely darkness.

This land contrasted sharply with the place of her birth, the desert that stretched to the unending horizon, or was broken with the stark red boulders that led to snowcapped mountains beyond her seeing. But this was a glorious place.

She burst into the clearing where Parker waited for them with a tolerant half smile on his lips. Sitting beside a boulder, he rested one hand on a raised knee. His boots were scuffed, his muscular legs confined by tight-fitting material. He had tipped his hat to the back of his head at a jaunty angle.

At the sight of him, she was swept by a heated dream wind.

Turning, for fear her expression might reveal her most secret thoughts, she gathered the youngsters into her arms.

"Oh, you have caught me!" she lied on a breathless laugh, all the more joyous because of Parker's presence.

"I knew I'd catch you," Kevin bragged. "I was one of the fastest kids in my class."

"Me, too," echoed Amy.

"You are both as fleet as the sheikh's messenger," she agreed, ruffling Kevin's hair and hugging Amy. "But now you must let me rest. I am too old for so much exertion."

Kevin looked at her critically. "You don't look so old to me."

"Ah, but I am. Hundreds of years old."

"Naw. Nobody's *that* old."

"Careful, son," Parker warned from his spot at the edge of the picnic blanket. "Women are a sensitive breed when it comes to their age."

Nesrin laughed again. "Come, let us have some lunch."

While she set the picnic basket in the middle of the blanket, Amy plunked herself down right next to Parker. He smiled and gave her a wink.

"We used to go on picnics with Mommy and Daddy," she said, her blue eyes turning into sad little saucers. "To an o-sis out in the desert."

"Oasis," Kevin corrected, selecting a piece of fried chicken and a canned soda from the basket. He found a place to sit with his back against a tree trunk.

"You miss your folks, don't you?" Parker said to Amy.

Chin quivering, she nodded. "But I like you, too, Uncle Parker."

He felt awkward as hell, and totally inadequate, but he wrapped his arm around her tiny little shoulders and gave her a hug. "Truth is, I miss your mother, too. She was a pretty special lady."

"She's in heaven now."

"Yep. But I figure she's still able to give me a swift kick in the butt if I mess up with you and your brother."

"You won't," Amy announced with considerable confidence. She squirmed away and dug through the picnic basket until she found her very own, favorite peanut butter sandwich. "You're the best uncle in the whole entire world. Mommy said so lots of times."

Parker glanced up at the sky—toward heaven, he supposed—and prayed he could live up to one small child's lofty expectations.

"DON'T GO WANDERING too far away," Parker ordered after the children had eaten their lunch and gotten bored with quiet conversation. "And watch yourselves around the creek. That current is a lot faster than it looks."

Agreeing to use caution, the children went off to explore along the creek bed, and Nesrin settled down next to Parker, gracefully folding her legs beneath herself. She was like a butterfly coming to rest, Parker mused. He envied her whimsical spirit even while he disapproved of her fanciful ways.

"*Hundreds* of years old?" he asked, remembering how she had claimed to be so ancient. "You really shouldn't fill the kids' heads with that kind of nonsense."

"And if it is true?"

"It's not, Nesrin. And you don't have to worry about getting deported. I've got a friend working on a green card for you."

A frown pleated her forehead. "Green card?"

"It'll make working for me legal."

She nodded, though Parker wasn't entirely sure she understood what he was talking about.

Wearing Marge's oversize jeans, she fiddled with the shimmering length of silk tied around her waist, shifting the tips uneasily between her fingers. "You are a most serious man, Parker, even when you seek a day of rest. Have you found no room for play in your life?"

"Not much," he conceded. Though he could easily imagine a few amusements he'd enjoy sharing with Nesrin. And, to his surprise, he was also beginning to enjoy hanging around with the kids. "My father didn't exactly believe in fun and games."

She raised her gaze to meet his. "He beat you?"

She looked so horrified, Parker took her hand. A foolish action, he immediately realized, but he didn't let go. Her slender fingers vanished within his much larger palm, soft flesh pressing against his calluses. It was no trick to imagine how her hands would feel touching him in intimate ways, and his body instantly responded to the tactile image.

He tried to ignore the feeling.

"Dad had the reputation of being the best damn general in the army—he still is—but he didn't believe in corporal punishment." Unable to stop himself, Parker toyed with her delicate fingers. Her bones felt fragile, almost ethereal. "On the other hand, he wasn't averse to making a raw recruit—or me—stand at attention for six or eight hours straight. In my case, right in front of the house where all the other kids could see me. He thought that built character."

"But that is terrible, to embarrass a small boy."

"That wasn't as bad as when he had me parade around the housing area with a sign on my back that said Punishment Detail."

"Ah, so these are the reasons you do not wish the children to live with their grandfather."

Those and a thousand more bitter memories. "You got it. I wouldn't want Kevin and Amy to go through that kind of hell."

Her dark eyes filled with unshed tears. "Where was your mother? Why didn't she put a stop to such cruelty?"

"She did what the general told her to do until a couple of years ago when she died. I always suspected unquestioned obedience had been part of the agreement when they got married." He shrugged, wondering why he was telling Nesrin all this. Normally he kept his past to himself. He didn't like dredging up painful memories. "There were a lot of strong men who didn't have the courage to cross my father. Mother didn't have a chance."

"But surely your father loved you, his son."

"He thought of me in the same way he thought of his troops. They were going to be the best damn soldiers in the world. I was his star pupil." The reality of those words, and Parker's subsequent failure, left a bitter taste on his tongue. "He accomplished one thing. When I finally got to the academy, it seemed like a girls' club."

"And now?"

"Since I messed up my ankle and had to take a disability retirement, I'm of no more use to my father. He's into perfection—and I don't qualify."

"Others might disagree."

He chuckled a low, disbelieving sound. "Truth is, I was almost relieved when I broke my ankle. The Dunlaps have been career army for generations. I was never sure when I got a promotion if it was because I'd earned it, or because someone thought it only right I follow in my old man's footsteps. Besides..." He looked around proudly. "This is my land. I've dreamed about owning a horse ranch since I was a kid. Now I've got to hang on to it."

She shook her head in sympathy. "Was your father as stern with your sister?"

"Mostly Dad ignored her when we were kids. It was Mother's job to teach her the important things he thought a woman needed to know—like how to pour tea for the officers' wives, and curtsy when she met foreign dignitaries. Marge didn't like it any better than I liked doing forty push-ups when I was two minutes late for dinner because my bike chain had busted."

"I'm sorry," Nesrin whispered, the words thickening in her throat. Even if her father had been weak, he had always been kind to her. She had been confident of his love. Surely he had not intended her any pain when he placed that desperate wager with Rasheyd.

She wished she could offer the same small comfort to Parker. Like the dark rain clouds that nuzzled the high mountain peaks beyond the creek, she wanted to rest her head on Parker's strong shoulder. Little wonder, given the cruelty that lay in his past, that Parker could not believe in the magic she knew to be true. Tragic, too, for in his own way she suspected he was a grand wizard who had not even begun to test his strength.

His gaze seemed to settle on her lips and she felt imperceptibly drawn toward him, in the same way an unseen wind moves grains of sand across a desert. Oddly, she felt a connection between the way he was looking at her and an unfamiliar heaviness filling her breasts.

Drawing a breath became difficult. In some strange manner, she needed to feel his lips pressed against hers. Softly. Warmly, she thought. But at some basic level she realized where such a dangerous action might lead her, and she let the thought slide away.

Withdrawing her hand, she glanced toward the creek. The absence of his warmth sent a shiver of longing through her body that she did not dare acknowledge.

She had never known the intimate touch of a man. Although she had feared what it would be like with Rasheyd, for centuries she had wondered how would it would be with another man. Someone she cared for.

From the darkness of her lamp she had envied those women for whom the experience had been pleasurable, and pitied those who had suffered in pain and silence. For the first time in all of her existence, she truly regretted she would never know such an experience herself. With Parker...

Over the murmur of the creek and the restless hum of the leaves in the highest branches, Nesrin could hear the sound of the children playing. Carefree sounds that made her think of the happy times she had spent in her village, of families laughing together.

"It would be a shame if you and the children would have to leave this lovely place," she said, thinking of the loan that so concerned Parker.

Determination weighed his brows into a straight line. "I'm not going to let that happen any more than I'll let the general take Marge's kids away. I take my promises seriously."

Before Nesrin could respond to his words, the timbre of the creek changed. Suddenly rough water tumbled more fiercely over the rocks.

A note of urgency cut into Kevin's voice.

"Amy! Hang on!" he shouted. "Uncle Parker... help!"

"What now?" Parker muttered, jumping to his feet and running toward the creek before the child's fear had fully registered in Nesrin's mind.

The creek had risen by two or three feet, the water licking angrily at rocks that had been dry only an hour ago. The current spun crazily, white foam spewing above the muddy stream. At the center of the creek, Amy had a precarious hold on the one remaining visible boulder.

"What happened?" Nesrin asked, shock and terror temporarily paralyzing her.

"Flash flood." Parker ran to his horse, which had been grazing nearby, grabbed a coiled rope and tied it securely to a tree at the water's edge. "I should have known those damn clouds were dropping rain up in the high country."

"I tried to reach her, Uncle Parker. Honest, I tried." The boy's jeans were wet to the waist, his young face a mask of fear. "I had a hold of her but she slipped away. I couldn't help it, Uncle Parker. I couldn't."

"I know, son." Parker yanked off one boot and then the other. "Stay here." Rope slung over his shoulder, he waded into the water. Almost immediately his feet slipped out from under him. He fought against the press of the current, righting himself and struggling on.

Amy's pleas for help could barely be heard above the roar of the water.

Helplessly Nesrin watched the swirling water. If only she was more confident of her powers, she might be able to save the child. More likely she would bring an even bigger wall of water crashing down on them all. She cursed her ineptness.

Before Parker could reach Amy, a wave of cruel white water snatched the child away from the scant protection of the boulder. She spun downstream, her head bobbing out of sight.

Nesrin sobbed her name. "Amy..."

Parker shrugged away from the rope and dived into the water, swimming after the child. The current caught him in the same tumbling, swirling foam that had sent Amy plummeting downstream.

Horrified that both Parker and Amy might drown, Nesrin dashed for the horses. She yanked Magnum's reins free. Mounting, she urged Parker's magnificent stallion into a thundering gallop that took them along the course of the stream. Tree branches slapped at her face and arms. She ignored them as she cast about in her mind for a way to save Parker and Amy, two people who had grown dear to her.

The trail veered away from the swollen creek, then back again. She caught a glimpse of Amy's tiny blond head, and heard her frightened cry.

Downstream, beyond the child, Nesrin saw a fallen tree stretched out above the creek. If only she could get there before the child did, perhaps there would be hope for saving her.

In her imagination, she whispered a command to the horse. *Go faster! Be fleet of foot!* Magnum responded with a burst of energy. He cut his way past trees and over the rocky ground as though he were a swiftly flying magic carpet.

She leapt to the ground beside the fallen tree, its ball of roots like gnarly fingers torn violently from the earth by an evil wind. As she scampered along the rough bark of the fir tree, and clambered over branches that tried to block her path, she ripped the strip of silken veil from her belt loops. She lay down and stretched as far as she could, dangling the veil above the water.

"Amy! Catch my veil." When the child failed to respond, Nesrin called again. "Look up, Amy! I'm here."

The unpredictable current swept Amy toward the far bank, out of Nesrin's reach. "No," she cried. "Come this way."

Though the fast-moving water raced beneath Nesrin's perch, everything else seemed to be happening in slow motion. The breeze catching and twirling the end of the veil. A wave of water shoving Amy back to the center of the creek. The sudden, welcome tug of the child's hand at the tip of the scarf.

"Hang on, sweet Amy. Hang on." Nesrin's perch was too precarious to pull the child to safety. Help would have to come from elsewhere.

A moment later Parker appeared in the water beside the child. Nesrin felt a surge of relief fully as powerful as the wall of water that had been sent down from the top of the mountain. Another emotion swept through her, as well, one she couldn't quite identify.

Nesrin gratefully relinquished her hold on the scarf as Parker assured Amy's safety.

Once Parker had his arm around Amy's waist, he swam for the shore. His muscles shrieked with fatigue. His battered body throbbed with a dozen bruises from collisions with hidden boulders. If it hadn't been for Nesrin's quick thinking, he might not have caught up with Amy in time to save her from drowning. Given the speed of the current, he had no idea how she'd managed to get downstream of the girl. He was simply grateful for her intervention and the clever use of her decorative silken scarf.

Breathing hard, and carrying Amy in his arms, Parker scrambled up the steep bank. He grabbed onto a clump of grass to pull himself the rest of the way to the top.

Nesrin was there to meet him. "Is the child all right?" she asked. The softness of concern filled her anxious brown eyes.

Amy coughed and clung to him more tightly.

He adjusted the child's position in his arms. "Except for swallowing half the river, sounds like she'll be fine," he said.

"And you?"

"Battered and bruised, but not beaten."

Nesrin brushed her fingertips to his cheek in a warm, all-too-brief caress. "I was worried...about you both."

No one had worried about Parker in a good many years—if ever. Somehow, in spite of his fatigue, her words made him stand a little taller. Which was saying something for a guy who was already a couple of inches over six feet. Nesrin certainly had a powerful effect on him. It was more than just sex, he realized—an unfamiliar combination of protectiveness and pleasure at simply being with her. He'd never felt like that with any other woman, certainly not his former wife.

Two horses crashed through the woods, Kevin mounted on one mare and leading the other.

"Did you get her? Is Amy okay?" He slid from the horse and raced to his sister.

Amy squirmed to get out of Parker's arms. The two youngsters hugged each other, and Parker remembered the times that he and Marge had had only each other's comfort to share. He cleared his throat of the lump that threatened to close off his breathing. Thank God he hadn't let Amy drown.

"I was tryin' to get you, Amy," Kevin said. "I swear I was."

"I was scared. You left me."

"I went for help. I had to, sis. I wasn't strong enough..."

Years of being on the receiving end of parental blame for the least infraction whipped through Parker's memory. He winced with each bitter recollection. Like the time he'd been protecting Marge from a school-yard bully and the kid had ripped Parker's shirt. Or when he'd loaned a friend his bike, only to have him leave it clear across town. He'd walked nearly ten miles that day to retrieve the darn thing. Not that his folks had ever appreciated any of his efforts.

Parker placed a reassuring hand on Kevin's shoulder. "You did the best you could, son. Your mom would have been proud of you."

The relief in the boy's eyes and the way Kevin stood a little straighter were a reward Parker hadn't expected. Maybe he shouldn't get in such a snit over the youngster's ponytail and scruffy shoes.

"Any kid who cares as much about his sister as you do is okay in my book," Parker said. He gave the boy a smile and got sort of a macho, one-of-the-guys grin in return. The exchange was a little stilted, at least on his part, Parker admitted, but it made him feel damn good. Maybe being a father wasn't so hard after all.

From the other side of the creek came the call of a stallion. The two mares shifted uneasily in response to Lucifer's invitation. Magnum snorted his displeasure.

"Come on, kids, Nesrin. Let's get on home," Parker said. At least the wild stallion hadn't gone too far from the ranch. There was still a chance he could be caught. But that effort would have to wait for another day. "We could all use some dry clothes."

"Hey, Uncle Parker, did you see Nesrin ridin' Magnum? Man, she made that horse fly."

Parker slanted her a surprised glance, belatedly realizing she'd ridden *his* mount rather than the gentle mare

Rusty had saddled for her. "Why did you come after us on Magnum instead of your own horse?"

"Because he was the fastest of the three," she explained.

He frowned. "Yeah, but he doesn't usually let anyone else ride him except me. I hand-trained him and he spooks real easy. He doesn't even like Rusty or one of the boys to saddle him."

"Perhaps he knew you were in trouble."

Maybe, but Parker wasn't quite sure he bought that possibility. More likely, Nesrin was simply a very skilled horsewoman.

"I mean the horse *really* flew," Kevin persisted. "Like his hooves didn't even touch the ground."

"Sounds like you've had too much excitement, boy. It's scrambled your brains."

"But I'm telling you—"

"Mount up, Kevin. The sun's going down and I'm starting to get cold in these wet clothes. Your sister, too. Let's move it."

Nesrin blew out a sigh. Had she really caused Magnum to fly? Or had it only been Kevin's fear and imagination that had made the horse appear to loft his hooves above the landscape?

Oh, rotten figs! If her incantations were more consistent, she could have some faith in her powers. As it was she didn't dare risk wishing too hard for anything. The results were too devilishly unpredictable.

Still, she thought smugly, she may well have levitated the horse. That was quite a trick. Almost as powerful as one Rasheyd might have conjured. And she had, only days ago, briefly levitated Amy...until Parker had startled her. The silverware spell had gotten out of hand, of course, emptying every drawer before she could halt the process.

If only her skills were more reliable...

FLYING HORSES? Nonsense.

By the time they returned to the ranch, Parker still hadn't figured out how Nesrin had beaten Amy to that downed tree. The more he thought about it, the more puzzled he became. He knew the path along the creek. It was rugged and winding. A rider couldn't possibly get up any speed, and if he tried, his horse would probably break a leg.

The only possible way would have been to fly. And he didn't believe that cockamamy idea for a second!

Dismounting at the corral, Parker gave his horse a quick once-over, running his hands over Magnum's withers and flanks, checking his legs. Not a scratch! Hell, he'd figure it out later.

He sent the kids into the house with Nesrin and unsaddled the horses.

In the barn he found Rusty staring glumly at a dismantled generator. If his hired hand had been trying to repair the old piece of equipment, it didn't look like things were going well.

Mentally calculating how much this problem was going to cost him, Parker hefted his saddle over the edge of a stall. He couldn't handle any extra expenses right now. To add to his worries, he knew if the bank fore-closed, they'd likely sell the ranch to a big conglomer-ate, an impersonal company that wasn't likely to keep three half-worthless old geezers like Rusty, Pete and Buck on the payroll. He didn't like the idea of the threesome being cut loose with no place to go.

"What's wrong?" Parker asked.

Rusty scratched at the fringe of hair at the back of his head. "Thought I'd do a little overhauling of this here generator, grease the bearings and such. It'd been awhile."

"And?" Parker encouraged.

"Well sir, after I got all done, I tried to fire her up and she just whined at me. Metal to metal, so to speak. So I took her all apart again."

Parker hunkered down to look at the parts strewn on the wooden floor. As mechanics went, Rusty was bet-ter at mucking stalls. "So what do you think is wrong?"

"Figure these here brushes are plum wore-out. I called into town. They ain't got replacements on hand. It'll be three, four days, maybe a week afore they can get some."

Fingering the part, Parker tended to agree with his hired hand's assessment of the problem . . . this time. When he'd bought the ranch there'd been lots of de-ferred maintenance apparent, some of which he hadn't taken care of yet. It looked like the generator had just moved to the top of the list. Fortunately, except for the expense, being temporarily without a generator wouldn't create a crisis. Commercial power was pretty reliable around here.

"Okay, let's order the replacements," Parker said. "Meanwhile, put the generator back together as best you can so we don't lose any parts."

"You got it, boss."

Parker headed back outside to bring in another saddle. He met Louanne at the barn door.

"Howdy, neighbor," she said. "Heard you folks had yourselves quite a picnic."

"I should have realized it was raining in the high country." He'd been distracted, he admitted. Nesrin had that effect on him. "We were lucky Amy didn't drown."

"Yep. Reckon so." Louanne fell into step beside him, her strides almost as long as his. "I was in to the feed store this morning, talking to Jasper. We was just jawing about this and that, and he was telling me 'bout some fellas who came by asking questions 'bout Marge."

He stopped in his tracks. "Marge?" Except for Louanne, and his hired hands, no one around here even knew about his sister.

"That's what Jasper said. A couple of middle-aged guys. Black hair. Mustaches. They were wearing black suits and asking special-like about your sister. One of the guys had himself a peculiar tattoo."

"How's that?" Parker lifted a saddle from the fence, and Louanne picked up the last one, rested it on her shoulder like a sack of potatoes and followed him back into the shade of the barn.

"Jasper said it looked to him like a little dinky garter snake wrapped around the guy's thumb. Kinda weird, don't you think?"

"There's no accounting for taste." He'd known a few drunken soldiers who'd ended up with worse tattoos after a night on the town.

"Thing is, they wanted to know where your ranch was."

"He tell them?"

"Jasper didn't like the looks of 'em. Thought maybe they were some kind of government inspector. He figures if they follow his directions, it'll take 'em two or three days to find the place."

Parker's lips twitched into a half smile. "Tell Jasper thanks next time you see him."

"I will. We both thought you'd want to know."

"I appreciate it." He wasn't sure who the two men might be, or their connection to Marge, but he had the uncomfortable feeling they might be from Immigration. Maybe someone had gotten wind of a stowaway in Marge's effects.

Or the two guys might be irate brothers in search of a missing sister.

In any event, he was planning to have a serious talk with Nesrin.

Chapter Five

The images flickering across the front of the box were quite a puzzle to Nesrin. Kevin had laughed when he found her peering at the back of the box, hoping to discover how all of those tiny people had gotten inside. He had vainly attempted to explain the box was a television, and those pictures she saw were nothing more than electronic dots racing across a screen.

She couldn't see any dots, she thought, raising her eyebrows. It was not nice for a young boy to make light of her ignorance, even if it was so.

Curling up at the end of the couch and pulling the long braid of her hair over her shoulder, she vowed someday she would catch those tiny people as they came and went from Parker's house. Then Kevin would know she could be as clever as he.

After their frightening ordeal at the creek that afternoon, the children had eaten and gone to bed early. The house was quiet now, save for the voices of the tiny people in the box. She liked to rest here in this pleasant room, with its comfortable furniture and a carpet as decorative as one that might have belonged to a sheikh. For nostalgic reasons, Nesrin had placed the brass lamp on a wide shelf above the rock fireplace. Parker had not objected.

She sensed his arrival in the room before she heard him. Perhaps all of those years in the lamp had made her senses particularly acute. At least, when it came to Parker that seemed to be the case. She caught his special masculine scent on the lightest movement of air, a mixture of leather and sunshine. Even from a distance, she became aware of his nearness from the heat that radiated from his body. And always, she felt drawn to him.

"Can we talk, Nesrin?"

She glanced up and smiled. "If you wish it."

In a few easy strides, he crossed the living room and pressed the button that made the box go dark. He had bathed before dinner and his sand-colored hair still curled damply at the nape of his neck. She remembered when he had released her from the lamp she had linked her fingers around the back of his neck and felt the spun gold of his hair. She wished she could relive the same experience again but knew she did not dare.

In her mind's eye, she saw herself in his arms. They would sway together in the same way she had seen men and women dancing inside the television. Parker would be strong, holding her tightly. And she would mold her body against his. Then he might press his lips to hers in what she had learned was a kiss. The music would swell, her heart flutter with joy.

It was a lovely image that teased through her mind, but when she blinked it was gone and Parker was frowning at her.

He stood in front of the television, his legs spread slightly apart, his arms folded across his chest. He appeared troubled, puzzled. And very stern.

He shook his head as though to rid himself of unwelcome thoughts.

Nesrin shifted uneasily on the couch. Surely he had not seen the vision of them dancing together.

He cleared his throat. "Is there anyone who might have known you were planning to come to the States?"

"I do not think so." She had not known so herself.

"Well, Louanne tells me there were a couple of guys in town asking about Marge. I figure they might have been looking for you."

Anxiety prickled along her spine. "What did they look like?"

"Dark hair, middle-aged."

Nesrin's eyes widened. "Did one have a long, beak-like nose and black eyes filled with evil?"

He shook his head. "I wouldn't know about that. But if there's somebody looking for you, I need to—"

"A tattoo?" Her voice hitched. "Did either of them have a tattoo on his thumb?" Nesrin fought a rising sense of panic.

"Yeah," he said slowly, a frown pressing his eyebrows into a straight line. "A snake. On his thumb."

Terror drove Nesrin to her feet. "It's Rasheyd! He's come after me!" By all that was holy, it was not fair.

She had done nothing wrong. She had not submitted to another. The wizard had no need to track her down like some rabid wolf stalking a helpless victim.

She shivered and hugged herself. "You must help me escape, Parker. I'll hide in the mountains. There must be a cave. Somewhere safe. I can't go back into the lamp. I can't..." Her voice trailed off into a shuddering sob. The thought of renewed darkness terrified her...that and the knowledge that if she were sent back into the lamp she would never see Parker again.

Parker did the only thing he could. He wrapped his arms around her and held her tight. She trembled against him, small and fragile, and needing his protection. In all of his years of facing danger, even leading young, untried troops, he'd never known anyone so thoroughly frightened. He wanted to find this Rasheyd character and flatten him. No one had a right to terrorize a woman this way.

And Nesrin, he realized, was at heart a brave woman. She'd traveled across the globe on her own. She'd ridden the wildest stallion without an ounce of fear. Somehow she'd managed to save Amy. And she damn well didn't deserve this kind of treatment from any man—even if it was her brother, or worse, a husband she hadn't told him about.

That last thought tightened a knot in his gut. He didn't want her to have a husband—estranged or otherwise. He wanted her all to himself. Permanently. His need to hold her, dance with her was so powerful he could almost imagine the feel of her in his arms, as though he were recalling something that had actually happened and not a dream inspirated by his frustration.

"Nesrin, you've got to tell me what's going on. I can't help you if you don't."

With a shuddering sigh, she lifted her face, and he used his thumbs to wipe tears from her cheeks. Her skin was warm and so soft he ached to do more than simply brush away a few tears.

"You will not ... believe me," she said.

"Try me."

She did.

She told him incredible things, slowly at first and then with more authority. He didn't for an instant doubt that she believed her wild tale. She was too wrapped up in the story to be faking such outrageous lies. But what sane person could believe in ancient curses, an evil wizard with a tattoo, emeralds and rubies, and being condemned inside a lamp for centuries?

"Just how many households have you been in?" he asked, trying to play along and at the same time glean information about who might be looking for her ... or Marge.

"Dozens. So many I have lost track. Sometimes, for long years at a time, the lamp was put away in some silent place. Perhaps a storeroom. I could not be sure."

"How come someone would buy the lamp and then not use it?"

"No flame would stay lit, for which I was very grateful. Had they burned a wick too long, I might not have survived."

Right. It probably would have shortened her life expectancy by a couple of hundred years. "So what did you do all this time?"

"When I was a part of a household—as I was with your sister—I listened very hard so I could learn their language. I speak several Arabic tongues, plus Turkish, German and, of course, English."

"Of course," he echoed. It all sounded so logical the way Nesrin told the story, but Parker knew damn well there wasn't a grain of truth in a word she'd said. There couldn't be. Though he was pretty darn sure this man named Rasheyd had traumatized her, Parker figured the rest of the story was her way of coping with painful memories. Sometimes men broke under fire and reacted in the same way. He could understand that.

She looked at him guilelessly. Lord, he wanted to protect her and make everything all right.

"You say this all started during the Crusades?" he asked. He'd been tracking her as she paced around the room, holding her when she became so overwrought she couldn't speak, and giving her room when she needed it.

"I believe that is what your historians have called that time. I know my people feared attacks from the infidels in the north."

"But you don't know the man looking for Marge is this Rasheyd fellow you're worried about. Not after nine hundred years, give or take a few centuries."

Her gaze darted around the room as if she expected a bogeyman to pop out of the woodwork. "Who else could it be?"

Parker didn't know, but he was damn well going to find out. He had a few connections who could tap the right sources. With the loan on the ranch about due and his father nipping at his heels for guardianship of the kids, Parker wasn't in any kind of a mood to tolerate another problem tossed in his lap. Particularly a nine-hundred-year-old problem.

After he convinced an exhausted Nesrin to go to bed, Parker picked up the phone and jammed in a long-distance number.

"Colonel Billingsly," came the gruff response at the other end of the line.

Parker instinctively snapped to attention, then relaxed. Military protocol was a thing of the past for him. "Hello, Bill. Hope I didn't wake you."

"Parker, you old son of a gun, it's past midnight here. Don't you know there's a time difference between Colorado and Washington?"

"Does that mean I've caught in you bed with some gorgeous blonde?"

"Redhead. Now what do you want?"

Parker chuckled to himself. Some things don't change, and the men of Special Forces had a tendency to live hard and fast, on or off duty. He used to be the same.

"A couple of guys have been in town asking questions about Marge."

"Your sister? I was really sorry to hear she'd died. An accident somewhere?"

"Yeah, and it's funny somebody would be asking questions about her now, here in Colorado. That's why I was hoping you could check them out for me."

"Sure. You think there's a problem?"

"Probably nothing serious." Assuming you didn't believe in wizards and curses, and Parker could get Nesrin a green card from his other buddy in the Immigration Service.

After Parker told Bill what little he knew of the two strangers, the colonel said, "So how's your ankle doing?"

"Never better."

"Man, I don't even know how you can walk around. You've got so many metal plates and pins in your ankle, you'd mess up a compass at ten paces."

"Going through an airport X-ray machine is always an interesting process."

"I bet." The colonel lowered his voice. "I'm still grateful, man. You know that, don't you?"

"It was my pleasure, Colonel." Free-falling a half mile in an effort to catch up with Bill when his chute failed to open had been an instinctive thing, not an act of courage. It had cost Parker a severely injured ankle and his military career. But it had saved a good man's life. That struck Parker as a fair trade-off. And in some ways he'd been relieved when he no longer had to prove he was general material like his father.

"Let me know when you find out something about those two guys," Parker said.

"Now can I get back to what I was doing?"

"Sure, buddy. Didn't mean to interrupt—"

An abrupt click terminated the phone call. Parker smiled and his thoughts traveled upstairs to Nesrin's bedroom. Damned if he didn't envy the colonel, but his preference would be for a brunette.

A HORN BLARED AND Nesrin winced.

She had not been out of the house for two days, not since she learned Rasheyd was looking for her. In fact, she still didn't want to be anywhere but in hiding. Parker had assured her, however, that there had been no sign of the two strangers in the past couple of days. So, in spite of everything, Nesrin found herself quite fascinated by her wild ride in Parker's motorized vehicle and her first visit to the nearby town of Gunnison.

In her village, the buildings had been constructed of mud and rough stone, those of the wealthy or powerful decorated with floral designs, or the outlines of animals. Here the structures were an interesting mix of white and pink and beige stucco. Those who would sell their wares had set up shop in long lines of buildings along the length of a wide boulevard, not tucking their businesses within a labyrinth of streets so narrow as to be nearly impassable.

She squeezed her eyes shut as Parker aimed his truck between two stationary vehicles that looked very much like the one she was riding in. When she heard no scraping of metal on metal, she opened her eyes again and heaved a relieved sigh. Modern transportation was far more frightening than crossing the desert on the back of a camel and certainly more rapid.

As they walked from Parker's truck to the store that offered food for sale, Nesrin held Amy's hand tightly and stayed close to Parker and Kevin. She would not want to be left on her own in this unfamiliar place. It was enough she had endured the journey here at such breakneck speed.

A slender young man with long, lank hair and wearing a soiled shirt approached Parker.

"Wonder if you can help me out, mister. My mom's real sick and I'm trying to get bus fare so I can go visit her in Denver. Just a dollar or two would help."

"Sorry." Parker kept on walking.

"Whatever you've got," the young man persisted. "A quarter, maybe."

Parker responded with a stony silence that horrified Nesrin. She hurried to catch up with him.

"Parker," she whispered, "you cannot ignore the beggar."

Halting before the door to the store, Parker said, "He's a panhandler, Nesrin. He probably has more money in his wallet than I do."

"But his mother—"

"That's a line, a complete prevarication so he can gain our sympathy."

"You do not know that, Parker."

"Sure I do. Every summer we get vagrants coming through here, all of them with sad stories that are a bunch of bull. They hang around the shopping center or down at the park. In the winter it's ski bums. There's an ordinance against panhandling, but it's not enforced unless they make a real nuisance of themselves."

He started to turn away, but she stopped him with the touch of her hand. "It is your holy duty to give the beggar a coin," she warned.

"You're kidding."

"No. In my village, beggars even give to beggars. It is the way of our people."

"Well, it's not my way. Giving those guys even a dime just encourages them."

She folded her arms across her chest in stubborn defiance. "Then I have no choice but to beg from others until I have a coin which I can give to him."

He scowled. "You wouldn't."

"It should not take me long. These people look very generous." She glanced at the passersby, most of the men dressed like Parker in jeans and cowboy hats. But none were as handsome, she observed. Nor did the sight of them make her heart skip a beat as it did whenever she caught a glimpse of Parker.

"I'd give you somethin'," Kevin said, "but I didn't bring any money with me."

"You are a sweet, kind boy, *unlike* your uncle," she said pointedly.

"We could go back to the ranch," Amy suggested. "I gots a penny bank at home."

Nesrin gave Parker a self-satisfied smile.

He looked incredulously at the threesome. "Look, guys, he's a bum. If he worked at a job as hard as he does at panhandling, he'd be worth a fortune."

Looping her arm around Kevin's shoulder, Nesrin said, "Would you children help me beg a few coins for the man? We do not want to keep your miserly uncle waiting too long, and I am sure—"

"No!" Parker dug into his pocket and handed her a fistful of coins. "You three are suckers, you know that? But give him the damn money and let's get on with our business. We can't hang around here all day."

"As you wish—" she stood on tiptoe to place a soft, teasing kiss on his cheek "—most generous and wise uncle of two fine young children."

"Yeah, right," he grumbled.

His face colored with a blush, and Nesrin had to suppress a smile. She suspected Parker had a more charitable heart than he cared to admit. He had, after all, made a home for Kevin and Amy, and taken her in when she had arrived so unexpectedly. Yes, in his gruff way, he was a good and kind man, she was sure of that.

Parker waited irritably while Nesrin delivered the handful of change to the vagrant. The foolish woman probably *would* have started begging if he hadn't given in to her whim. And don't you know she would have had a purse full of money in minutes. Every guy who'd walked by had taken his own sweet time ogling her. They were far too interested in the sway of her slender hips, and the contrasting motion of the long braid that hung down her back. Parker didn't like those lingering perusals, not one damn bit. If he hadn't wanted to keep an eye on her himself, he would have left her back at the ranch. But Rusty and the boys had come into town on their own, and there was nobody to watch out for her.

Next time he'd figure a way to leave her at home. A woman like Nesrin needed to be protected from these mountain cowboys. They weren't exactly shy when it came to taking advantage of innocent young women.

He rubbed his hand on the spot she had kissed. Not shy about innocent, nine-hundred-year-old women, either, if you believed her screwy story. Which he didn't.

He glanced around the parking lot. No sign of two out-of-place strangers here. Maybe they'd lost interest in tracking down Marge... or Nesrin. He didn't even want to consider the possibility that someone was after the kids. Or that his father had put a misbegotten pair of inept private detectives on his tail to prove he wasn't worthy of parenting the youngsters.

It would help if he'd get word back from his buddy in Special Ops.

When Nesrin returned from her mission of mercy, he cupped her elbow, and ushered her and the kids into the store. It wasn't safe to leave her loose on her own. No telling what kind of mischief she might get into.

He sent the kids off with the rest of his change to play at the video games and grimly began the grocery shopping.

In the canned-good aisle, Nesrin clapped her hands with glee. "Look, Parker, the picture tells you what is inside the can."

His lips twitched from a surly scowl to a half smile. "Yeah, makes shopping easier that way."

"So very clever of you Americans. And you have so many choices!" she exclaimed. All but dancing from one side of the aisle to the other, she selected an assortment of vegetables, dropping one can after another into the cart.

His smile grew a little wider. Nesrin was so excited about her visit to the grocery store, he couldn't even complain when in the next aisle she picked a dozen different boxes of cereal to pile into their already heaping shopping cart.

But when she came to an abrupt halt in front of the pet food he wondered why.

"What's wrong?" he asked.

She looked pale, her delicate features clouded with worry. "Do you eat . . . cats and dogs?"

It took him an instant to puzzle out what she was talking about. Then he realized there were pictures of dogs or cats on their respective pet food cans, just as there had been pictures of beans on the cans in the vegetable aisle.

It took all of his willpower not to laugh out loud and he really didn't want to make her feel the fool. She'd obviously never been in a grocery store before. He imagined he wouldn't do any better trying to manage a herd of camels, or whatever it was her family had done for a living in her homeland.

"No, sweetheart, that's food *for* dogs and cats, not ground-up pets. Trust me."

She still looked a bit skeptical as she warily moved down the aisle. Parker found himself wishing he could teach her more than just the ropes of grocery shopping, delights of a far more intimate nature.

Not a good plan, he told himself. For all he knew, given her bizarre story about being locked up in a lamp for nine hundred years, she might be an escapee from the local psycho ward.

In the meat department, she peered at the cellophane-wrapped packages. "I do not see any sheep's brains," she complained. "I had wanted to prepare my specialty for you. With dates, of course."

He silently thanked the butchers for their fortuitous omission.

"Wrong season," he assured Nesrin, hustling her toward the produce department.

At the fresh corn, they came on Rutherford Mildon, the man who had ordered the mustangs from Parker. He appeared to be sorting carefully through the bin in order to select the specific ears of corn best suited to expanding his size fifty-six waist.

"Well, howdy, Parker," he said. "How's it going with the mustangs?"

"Right on schedule. I've rounded up your twenty, plus some extras. We're working our way through saddle-breaking them now. Ought to have them in good shape with time to spare."

"I'm almost sorry to hear that, boy."

Parker frowned. "Why's that?"

"Well, now—" Rutherford dropped two ears of corn into an already full plastic bag "—there's this fella' up in Wanita Hot Springs who's selling his mares for near half the price of yours."

"We've got a contract, Rutherford."

"I know that." He dropped the sack into his burgeoning grocery cart. "Never broke my word yet, and don't intend to start now. Still…if for some reason you cain't deliver them horses on time, it shore wouldn't hurt my pocketbook none."

"I'll deliver, Rutherford. You can count on it." The future of Parker's ranch depended on it.

As Parker was about to put the groceries into the back of the truck, Nesrin said, "Could we walk through the town? It seems such an interesting place."

"There's really not much to see."

"Please, Uncle Parker," Kevin pleaded. "There's a video store down the street. Maybe they've got some cool games."

Amy gazed up at him with big melt-your-heart blue eyes. "I saw an ice-cream store," she said, her sweet request another tie that wrapped Parker around her little finger.

The three of them were ganging up on him. Again.

Oh, what the heck! Their first visit to town ought to be something special.

So Kevin rented a month's worth of video games, and Amy got her ice cream. To his surprise, Parker discovered he liked hanging around with the kids. They were smart as little whips—good enough to keep him on his toes—and they saw life as still full of possibilities. It made him realize how jaded he had become over the years.

Even so, as they headed back toward the truck, Parker wondered at his lack of firm discipline with the youngsters. Just because the kids had lost their parents didn't mean he had to give in to their every request.

Just this once, he assured himself. Then he'd start being strict with them, though not as demanding as his father had been, he promised himself.

In front of a pair of swinging doors, Nesrin came to a halt. There was music coming from inside. She heard laughter and detected the thick scent of tobacco mixed with the aroma of fermented grains. Suddenly she was swept with memories of dancing for her father and his friends. They had applauded wildly. For once, her father had been proud of her.

"What is this place?" she asked, trying to peer under the swinging doors.

"It's a bar. The High Mountain Saloon." Parker slid his arm around her waist and hurried her past the entrance. "A seedy honky-tonk filled with cowboys. You don't want to go in there."

She glanced back over her shoulder. No, she supposed she did not want that. But she did wish she could do something that would make Parker proud of her.

She had been troubled because he disbelieved all that she had told him about her past. She'd seen the doubt in his eyes and that worried her. How could he match his own formidable powers against Rasheyd if he did not recognize the strength of his adversary? And she feared there would come a time, in order to protect her from the wizard, that Parker might place himself in danger. Though her life was of little value, she did not want him to be injured...or worse, condemned to spend eternity in darkness as she had been.

By the time Parker got Nesrin and the kids back to the truck, he was fit to be tied.

It was bad enough every guy on the street had tossed an appreciative look in Nesrin's direction. And worse that she was so damn friendly she smiled back at every one of them. But the thought that she'd wanted to wander into a low-life bar had been the limit. Forget that Parker had spent a good many hours in that same saloon before she and the kids had arrived at his ranch. He knew what went on in there. How the guys talked. And what was on their little pea-brained minds.

The same damn thing that was on his mind.

If he had good sense, he'd bed her, brand her—metaphorically speaking, of course—and make damn sure every cowpoke in the county knew she belonged to him.

He wouldn't do that. It wouldn't be fair to Nesrin. But he was damn well tempted.

He yanked open the truck door for the kids.

"Uncle Parker, could we—"

"No!"

At his sharp retort, both kids came close to jumping out of their skins. Parker cursed himself. He didn't normally let himself slip so far out of control. And there was no reason he should take his frustration out on the kids.

He beat Nesrin to the passenger side of the truck, capturing her between the heated metal and the twin barriers of his outstretched arms. He was standing close to her, too close, and he caught her erotic scent, both foreign and tantalizing. Jeans had never looked so good on a woman. So damn sexy.

"Parker?" she questioned.

"We need to talk." His voice scraped roughly along his throat.

"Again?"

"Yeah."

Resting her small, delicate hands on his chest, she looked at him quizzically. "About what?"

About how he wanted to make love with her. Here. In the middle of town. With her propped on the fender of his truck. And how he didn't want any more cowboys looking at her without knowing she belonged to him.

Sweat beaded his upper lip. Nesrin wasn't the crazy one. He was. Crazy jealous.

"About..." He swallowed hard. Frantically he searched for a way out of the mess he'd gotten himself into. A way to cool down, when what he wanted was to feel the fire he sensed lurking behind Nesrin's innocent eyes. "About how to cook some of the stuff we bought at the grocery store."

"I had thought to ask Louanne."

"Good. Right. She can help you."

With the same force of will drilled into him by his father and the academy, Parker commanded himself to step back. He wasn't going to lose control. Not here. Not in front of the kids and half the town.

He would have moved, too, if he hadn't seen a spark of unadulterated curiosity in Nesrin's dark eyes. *Heated interest,* he mentally corrected. She was no more immune to him than he was to her. Hell, there wasn't any vaccination known to man that would stop the electricity that leapt between them.

His gaze swept her face, her finely sculpted cheeks and the sensuous curve of her lips. How could he get this riled up about a woman he hadn't even kissed? Not really. But he'd certainly thought about it enough.

"Parker..." Her voice was a low, sultry whisper that teased his overheated libido. "Are we going to stand here much longer?"

"You got a problem with that?"

"I think the children would like to go home."

Silently swearing at himself, he dragged his gaze from Nesrin's face and stared beyond the facades of the shopping center, to the shimmering blue-white sky beyond. He tamped down the raging desire that had him thinking like a wild man. His fingers flexed.

"Parker?"

This time there was a trace of fear in her voice, and who could blame her. It was enough to bring Parker blinking back to his senses.

For a moment he fingered the long, silken strands of her dark hair, then he shoved away from the truck to release her from the prison of his arms. He opened the door. "Let's get going," he ordered, turning away before he could change his mind.

Nesrin sat with her hands folded in her lap during the silent ride back to the ranch. The children seemed equally subdued. Something had happened when Parker had trapped her beside the truck. There'd been a change between them, a rising of tension like ropes pulled taut on a tent. Nesrin found the sensation both unnerving and exhilarating.

She had never felt more feminine. Not even when she danced. Only Parker had made her feel this riotous need for something more.

The need to *submit*.

That realization terrified her. To want something so much, and know insufferable agony would result, was a greater cruelty than she had ever imagined. A shiver of fear stroked through her insides. She would have to remain very strong in order to wage a successful battle against that which was her own weakness.

As they reached the ranch, Nesrin turned, sensing a sudden alertness in Parker she had not previously observed. His posture had gone rigid; his gaze darted from house to barn and back again as he slowed the truck to

a stop well away from his usual parking spot. Tension
rippled a muscle in his jaw and tightened his forehead.

There was something wrong.

Fear fluttered through Nesrin's middle.

Rasheyd!

Chapter Six

Ten years of service in Special Forces gave a man a sixth sense for danger.

Parker's kicked in with a vengeance the minute he drove into the ranch yard. It was like an invisible storm of static electricity raising the hairs on the back of his neck. The sudden awareness was so strong he felt like a porcupine.

Maybe it was the way the mustangs were milling erratically around the corral. Or maybe because Rusty's ol' barn dog was on his feet moving when he should have been resting in the sun.

Parker pulled the car to a quiet stop in front of the house. He switched off the ignition.

"I want you guys to stay right here," he ordered in the tone he used to command troops. "In the car. Don't move until I tell you."

Going as rigid as plebes at their first inspection, they didn't argue.

He slid out of the car. Soundlessly he closed the door. His senses were at full alert, his gaze sweeping the terrain. There was something wrong, and his mind flashed on the swarthy characters who had been asking questions about Marge.

A muscle rippled at his jaw. Years ago he'd given up carrying a weapon. There shouldn't have been a reason to on a horse ranch in the Rockies. Except for snakes. And he suspected there was a snake of the two-legged variety lurking somewhere nearby. Maybe more than one.

In this case, his hands and a good deal of stealth would have to be weapon enough. There wasn't time to get inside the house, get a gun from the locked rifle rack in the den, and then go in search of whoever had trespassed on his land.

From the back of the house he heard the thwack of the screen door slamming. Seconds later, before Parker could make it to the rear porch, a motor revved. A motorcycle, by the sound of it, a powerful one.

The guy on the bike rounded the corner of the house slowly. Until he saw Parker. Then, in a panic, he twisted the throttle, gunning the engine and sending gravel spewing off the back tire.

Lowering his shoulder, Parker made a dive for him. He connected in a satisfying collision that sent the pair of them crashing to the ground along with the bike, wheels spinning. The motorcycle whipped around like a mammoth, writhing snake. Parker twisted out of the way, then pinned the trespasser.

He lifted the cyclist's tinted helmet visor.

"The damned panhandler from town! What the hell are you doing here?"

Recognition flashed across the young man's face. "Hey, man, I didn't know this was your place."

Fisting the panhandler's collar, Parker lifted him to his feet. He couldn't have weighed more than a hundred twenty-five pounds. Scrawny and younger than he had realized, the kid probably hadn't seen his eighteenth birthday yet. Definitely wet behind the ears. A runaway, Parker suspected, though he couldn't guess from what, given the expensive bike he was riding. "Just whose place did you think you were breaking into?"

"I didn't know. Honest, I just heard some guys talkin'. You know, like this place might be a good mark."

"Be a little more specific, buddy, or you'll find yourself with a couple of broken arms." The kid was already terrified, but a little rough talk wouldn't hurt. "What'd they say?"

"They said some stuff about emeralds."

"Emeralds?"

"Yeah, you know. Jewels. Like you had a bunch of jewels stashed around here."

Not likely, but the reference to emeralds sent a prickle of apprehension down Parker's spine. Nesrin had said... "What did these guys you're talking about look like."

"I don't know. Kinda foreign. They had accents."

"So you were hanging around, eavesdropping, and you just *happened* to hear something about emeralds?"

"Well, kinda..." the kid hedged. "They sorta gave me a few bucks to come check out the place."

"Check out?"

"Yeah, you know. They wanted me to see how many hands you've got, if there's an alarm system. That kinda thing."

The kid had been casing the place, Parker realized, and that made him all the more anxious about the men who were snooping around town. He was about to ask the kid more questions, but Nesrin hadn't stayed put as she'd been ordered.

"You?" she asked incredulously, staring at the young man. "Did I not give you enough coins?"

"Yes, ma'am, you were real nice. I was just trying to tell your old man that I didn't know this was your place." Fearfully the kid's watery gray eyes darted from Nesrin back to Parker. "Shoot, I wouldn't hit on somebody who'd already given me some bread."

"Bread?" Nesrin questioned. "But I thought you wanted money so you could go visit your mother."

"It's an expression," Parker said. "I'll explain later."

"But he was going to take a bus," she persisted. "Why would he do that when he has a perfectly good machine that would take him anywhere he wanted to go?"

"Nesrin! Will you let me handle this."

She folded her arms across her chest and nailed the panhandler with a withering look. "In my country, beggars do not lie."

Parker rolled his eyes. "All right, kid, what did you manage to filch from inside the house?"

"Nothing, really."

"Let's see it."

The young man shrugged out of his backpack, opening it for Parker's inspection. Nesrin peered over his shoulder.

"Cans of soup?" Parker asked. "That's it?"

"Couple of apples." The kid hung his head, staring at the scuffed toes of his work boots.

Parker wasn't quite sure what to believe. The kid certainly wasn't a hard-core criminal, and there sure wasn't anywhere on the motorcycle to hide a computer or TV. Outside of that, there wasn't much of value in the house that could be stolen. He rarely kept cash on hand.

He made a perfunctory search of the pack, then righted the motorcycle so he could check the saddle-bags. He came up empty as far as any stolen merchandise. In fact, if the contents of the saddlebags represented the kid's entire worldly possessions, it didn't stand for much.

"Can I go now?" the boy asked.

"Yeah, I guess."

He straddled his bike and tested the throttle.

Nesrin tried to take the backpack from Parker, but he held back.

"He is hungry, Parker." Her voice was low and confidential.

"He lied about needing bus fare," he reminded her. And was probably setting them up for a robbery, he mentally added.

"I know." Her fingers flitted across his chest, brushing imaginary dirt from his shirt. "And you are a most generous man who does not hold a grudge."

He caught her fingers, like trapping the fragile wings of a hummingbird. "There's a sucker born every day."

"And only rarely does a truly good man appear. Like you, Parker."

He knew her words were flattery, said so she could get her softhearted way. But something in her eyes made him a believer, if only long enough that he tossed the pack to the kid.

"Get outta here," he ordered gruffly.

"Yeah. Sure. Thanks."

The kid gunned the bike, and the motorcycle raced away, an elongated cloud of dust rising as he headed toward the highway.

Rusty's lop-eared old dog finally decided to bark a warning.

More responsive to Parker's orders than Nesrin, Kevin and Amy piled out of the truck after they sensed everything was all clear.

"Keep the kids busy for a few minutes," Parker told Nesrin. "I want to check inside."

"You think there may still be someone—"

"Just a precaution."

"I want to go with you."

"Stay with the kids." He looked her squarely in the eyes. Damn, she was gorgeous, a rare combination of seduction and innocence. "I mean it this time."

Since the hair on the back of his neck had settled down, he figured it was safe enough to leave Nesrin and the children while he checked out the interior of the house. He wanted to get a look at what the panhandler had been up to inside besides snitching cans of soup. And he didn't want the kids underfoot.

He had just about finished reconnoitering, and finding that apparently nothing else had been touched, when he heard Rusty's truck rattling up to the house. He checked out the window just to make sure.

The phone rang.

"Hello, son, how are you?"

"Dad!" Parker's gut clenched. Talk about lousy timing. "Where are you?"

"Still in the Philippines making arrangements for the change-of-command ceremony and my official retirement."

Thank God he wasn't calling from somewhere in the States. Parker wasn't sure he was ready to deal with his father just yet, not where the kids' guardianship was concerned.

"Thought I'd check to see how you're getting along with my grandchildren."

"Fine, sir, just fine. They're adjusting real well to the ranch."

"Don't let 'em settle in too well, son. I've got big plans for the children. I've been investigating some prep schools for Kevin—"

"Dad, that's a little premature. They haven't even adjusted to not having parents yet. I don't think we ought to be sending—"

"You let me take care of things, young man. After all, I'm the one who has been a parent before. I think I know what's best, don't you?"

Hell, no, but it wasn't easy to tell the general anything. "We'll talk about it later, sir."

"All right. Tell the children stiff upper lip and I'll see them in a couple of weeks. Then I'll take them off your hands."

Parker's objection was cut off by the click of the phone.

He'd just speared his fingers through his hair in worried frustration when the damn phone rang again.

"Yeah," he barked.

"Parker, it's Louanne," announced the agitated voice on the other end of the line. "Those characters I told you about who were asking questions in town—"

Parker's sixth sense went back on alert. The ones who the panhandler had been doing his little job for? Men who thought there were emeralds stashed somewhere on his ranch?

"They're on their way out to see you. They weren't real happy about Jasper sending them off on a wild-goose chase."

"They hurt him?"

"Scared him is all, I think."

"Okay, I'll take care of things from here."

"Watch yourself, Parker. They're mean ones. I can feel it in my bones."

"I'll be careful."

Hanging up the phone, he also knew he had to take care for Nesrin and the kids. If Bill from Special Ops had gotten back to him, he'd have some idea of what he was dealing with. As it was, he was flying blind. There could be a dozen different legitimate reasons for someone to be after Nesrin, reasons that didn't have anything to do with a curse. Or emeralds. There might even be justifiable cause for following up on Marge's death.

But he wasn't going to take any chances. Not when he'd just caught someone burglarizing his house, however ineptly. And not with guys who liked to use intimidation to shove folks around.

From the gun case he got his Baretta and tucked it into the back of his jeans, handy but out of sight beneath his shirt. For added protection, and possibly surprise, he slid a sheathed knife down into the side of his boot.

Outside, he found Nesrin telling Rusty and the boys about the intruder.

He interrupted. "Rusty, I want you and the boys to get back in the truck, and take Nesrin and the kids over to Louanne's place."

"Now?" Rusty asked.

Pete gave the house a quick look, as though the danger might be coming from there. "Thought Miz Nesrin said there weren't nobody left inside."

"There isn't. But we're about to have company. A couple of guys who like to ask questions."

Nesrin gasped.

Buck hitched up his pants, ready for a fight. "One of us oughta stay here with you."

"No, I'll be fine. I want you to go the back way to Louanne's," Parker insisted. "And stay out of sight." These three old duffers would be more hindrance than help in a fire fight.

"You got it, boss," Rusty agreed.

"One more thing. You still know how to use that rifle?" With a jerk of his head, Parker indicated the hunting rifle mounted across the back window of Rusty's truck.

"Sure do. I kin pick a gnat off'n the back of a deer at a hundred paces."

Parker wasn't all that confident, since he figured Rusty couldn't see that far. Hopefully an intruder wouldn't realize that if he was facing the business end of the rifle. "Is it loaded?"

"Will be, soon as I kin get to it." Picking up on Parker's urgency, Rusty climbed into the truck. His cohorts went to round up the children, who'd wandered off to inspect the horses in the corral.

The blood had drained from Nesrin's face. "Is it..." She mouthed the word *Rasheyd?* as though she were afraid to speak his name aloud.

"I don't know, Nesrin. I won't know till they show up." And he wasn't going to say a word about emeralds. No need to get her upset. "You'll be safe. Louanne and the boys will watch out for you."

"You shouldn't be here alone. He is very powerful—"

"I'm trained for this. If anyone else was here it'd be a distraction."

"There are two of them," she whispered, fear making her voice thready, "and you are only one."

"But I'm tough, sweetheart. Trust me."

Her chin trembled. "I'll stay. I don't want you to be—"

Parker didn't have time to argue. So he did what he'd been wanting to do all day. Hell, what he'd been wanting to do since she first fell out of the back of his truck into his arms—quirky, beautiful and sexy as any woman he'd ever seen.

He kissed her.

Long and hot and hard. When she drew a quick breath, he took advantage of the opportunity, sliding his tongue into her open mouth. She tasted like the sweetness of honey, the heat of a summer day. And innocence. He felt starved for her flavor and drank it in.

After a startled moment, she made a little sound of pleasure and relaxed against him. With his big arms wrapped around her, she seemed no more than a wisp of a woman, but *all* female. Her breasts were small pressing against his chest, the gentle curve of her buttocks was the perfect place to rest his palm. He wanted to hold her like this for a long time, and keep on kissing her until they were both senseless with the fierce need that was already building in his veins.

But with uninvited guests about to arrive, she was a dangerous distraction. And he didn't want to put her at risk.

"Go," he ordered roughly, even as he pressed another soft kiss to her lips. "I'll call Louanne when it's all clear."

In her dark eyes he saw dazed surprise, and behind that the heat of a hunger that nearly matched his own.

Taking her shoulders, he turned her toward the truck.

Wordlessly, as though suffering from shock, she climbed into the back with Pete and Buck; the children were up front.

Her eyes never left his as the truck drove away. Her expression was heated with unfulfilled sexual needs and haunted by confusion.

Not until the truck was out of sight over a rise did Parker exhale the breath he'd been holding. Never had he been quite so shaken by a kiss. She was some kind of woman. And before this was over, Parker vowed they would share more than a kiss. Caution be damned!

HE WAS STILL CONSIDERING the sensual possibilities five minutes later when he heard the sound of a car approaching from the highway. He waited on the porch, nice and easy, his weight evenly distributed on the balls of his feet. He didn't want to telegraph his heightened state of readiness.

The two guys in dark suits got out of the car. With their toothy smiles and black slicked-back hair, they looked like salesmen trying to con him into buying a capped oil well in Kuwait.

"Major Dunlap?" the tall, slender one asked. He had a narrow, hooked nose and eyes as black as his suit. A wispy mustache curved above thin lips.

"It's *mister* now. I'm a civilian."

"Yes, of course." He extended his hand and Parker noted the swirl of a tattoo around his thumb. "I'm Mishal Ibrahim, and this is my associate, Tajir Gaddoumi."

Parker felt a certain amount of relief that neither of them were named Rasheyd. And they both appeared to be very much men of the twentieth century. "Gentlemen." After shaking hands with Ibrahim, he nodded to the second man. "What can I do for you?"

They produced some official-looking IDs and handed them over to Parker.

"We are from the Ministry of Antiquities," Ibrahim said. "We understand you have recently received a shipment of several crates from the Middle East."

"My sister's personal effects." Parker studied the IDs, not that it did him much good. He couldn't read a word of Arabic. The government seals looked legitimate, though, and the photos were definitely of the two men standing in front of him. Trouble was, he wouldn't know a forgery from the real thing. He supposed he ought to feel grateful these slick characters weren't sent by his father to investigate his parental skills with the kids.

"Ah, yes, the death of your sister and her husband was a shameful tragedy. We have reason to believe, however, that certain items of historic importance to our country were inadvertently shipped along with your sister's personal effects."

"Really? What kinds of things?"

"As you might well imagine, we are not entirely at liberty to—"

"Look, buddy, as far as I know everything that was shipped here, my sister came by honestly. Now, if you've got a problem with that, I suggest you find yourself a judge. If you get a court order, I'll let you browse through my sister's things. I'll even hand over anything that rightfully belongs to your country—assuming you can prove it in a court of law. Meanwhile—" he handed the IDs back to Ibrahim "—I don't plan to extend western hospitality to anybody who tries to push my friends around. Or asks a punk kid to check out my security system. Got that?" He used his greater height and weight to do a little intimidating of his own.

The two men stepped back in unison, the silent partner of the two looking more edgy by the moment.

"As you wish, Mr. Dunlap. I had hoped we might reach an amicable arrangement, perhaps a small reward for your assistance in returning—"

"I'm not interested."

"Yes, well..." The duo retreated toward their car. "Perhaps we will be able to find some other way to persuade you."

"I doubt it." Under no circumstances would he let those creeps go through Marge's things. She might have picked up something at a thieves' market that had some modicum of value, but he couldn't imagine she'd gotten hold of an "antiquity" like these guys claimed.

As Parker watched the car drive off, he wondered what the Arabian equivalent of a three-dollar bill might be. He figured those two guys qualified.

They had, however, piqued his interest.

In the back of the barn where he'd stored most of Marge's things, he went through the crates again. Carefully this time, trying not to let nostalgia gain a grip on his emotions. He didn't want to think about how much his sister had meant to him; how much he hated knowing their connection, however tenuous, had been forever severed.

Tears thickened in his throat. "I miss you, Marge, and I swear to you I'll do a better job of raising your kids than Dad did with us."

Nothing in the odds and ends that she had collected looked like a valuable antiquity, any more than the beat-up old lamp that Nesrin kept on the mantel in the living room looked worth more than a couple of bucks at a garage sale. And there sure weren't any emeralds that he could see.

He had the feeling his visitors had been tracking the wrong crates.

DISTRACTEDLY, NESRIN watched Kevin and Amy playing in Louanne's big swimming pool. She felt as buoyant as the children in the water. Her lips still tingled, and her heart had not yet slowed to a regular beat. Parker was clearly the man responsible for her agitated state.

"Girl, you surely do look like you're off on cloud nine." Louanne set a tray with a pitcher of lemonade and glasses on the table beside the pool. "You worried about Parker?"

Instinctively Nesrin's fingers touched her lips. "He said he would be fine."

"Reckon he will be." Louanne looked at her curiously. "You 'n' that boy gettin' along these days?"

"Oh, yes." Nesrin sighed. She stared off into the distance where the afternoon clouds were building against the mountain peaks. Dark, threatening clouds, so in contrast to her lighthearted mood.

"Let me take a guess. That man kiss you goodbye afore he sent you over here?"

Guilty heat crept up Nesrin's neck. "Oh, yes, it was a very nice kiss." Warm and wonderful, and very demanding. She had never expected to experience anything quite so exciting.

"I figured as much. Imagined it wouldn't take long for a girl like you to tumble head over teakettle in love with a man like Parker. He's some kinda hunk."

"In love?" Nesrin turned abruptly to Louanne. The possibility of *love* was far too dangerous for her to contemplate. She was already troubled enough by the thought of where one kiss might lead. "I do not think so."

"You surely do have all the symptoms, honey. Sorta glassy eyed and floating on air. I ought to know. Been there a few times myself."

"You have?"

"Sure have. Buried three husbands, rest their souls, and loved everyone of 'em to pieces. Wouldn't mind finding number four, either, if I get the chance." Louanne smiled wistfully. "It's magic, pure and simple, when you fall in love."

"I do not believe Parker believes in magic." Nor, in this case, should she.

"Of course not, honey. Men never do until some good woman comes along and shows 'em different." She patted Nesrin's hand in motherly fashion. "Love's the most powerful magic of all."

"Do you think so?" More powerful than Rasheyd's curse? she wondered.

"Absolutely. Why, I'm a firm believer that love can do the darnedest things. Move mountains, if need be."

"Among my people it would take a great wizard to have such power."

Louanne laughed, a deep, full-bodied sound. "Shoot, nothing to it in these parts. Personally, I wouldn't hang around with a man on any other terms." She took a long drink of tea. "No, sirree. I'd never settle for less with a man than knock-your-socks-off love. Otherwise a woman would just plain shrivel up to nothing."

Nesrin looked down at her feet. She didn't wear socks, only a slender gold chain around one ankle. But if she did, she was sure her socks would have slipped from her feet when Parker had kissed her. The feeling had indeed been that powerful.

She wondered if it had been the same for Parker.

"If a woman loves a man," she asked, "how can she get the man to love her in return?"

"Not much you kin do. It plain happens or it don't. And if it don't, it's a misery, I'll tell you that. You feel like you're not much more than chopped liver."

Chopped liver? Nesrin sighed, aware she was not always able to fully understand Louanne's colorful descriptions. She desperately wished she was not falling in love with Parker. It would make it all the more difficult not to submit to him. And if the other choice was to feel like ground-up innards, she certainly did not want that.

But perhaps Louanne was right. The magic of love might be powerful enough to protect her from Rasheyd's curse. But believing that might pose the ultimate risk, for if Louanne was wrong, the rest of eternity trapped in a lamp would be Nesrin's destiny. Particularly if Parker did not love her in return.

She shuddered at the thought, even while she watched the children romping in the pool.

"Did you know Parker's father wants to take the children away from him?" Nesrin asked her friend.

"Shoot no, I didn't know that. It'd purely be a shame to move those poor youngsters again, 'specially since they seem to be settling in real nice-like."

"When I first heard, I was very angry. I even thought to cast a spell on the man, something like filling his belly with crawly green worms, but I was not sure Parker would be pleased."

Louanne barked a laugh. "For such a sweet little thing, you surely do have a mean streak, honey. I reckon it'll be enough if you just be there when Parker needs you. Chances are he can convince his old man not to interfere with things as they stand."

"I hope that is true," Nesrin agreed as the portable phone rang on the table beside them.

Louanne answered, and after a moment announced, "Parker says the coast is clear."

"Is he all right?" Nesrin asked.

"Fit as a fiddle, he says. Guess we'll have to round up those no-good hired hands of his to take you on home."

"Aw, gee," Kevin complained from the pool. "Can't we stay here? I'm not done swimming yet."

Amy echoed the same sentiments.

Nesrin hesitated. "I don't know, children. Your uncle—"

"Oh, let 'em stay," Louanne insisted with an easy wave of her hand. "My grandkids live so far away they're not making very good use of this pool. And I've got me a big pot full of fresh-made spaghetti sauce boiling on the stove. Bet these youngsters could give it a taste test before I seal some up in them jars."

"Hey, yeah." Kevin's eyes grew wide in eager anticipation.

"In fact, let the youngsters stay the night. It gets pure lonely around here sometimes, and I bet you and Parker could use a little time off for yourselves."

Kevin boosted himself out of the pool. "Louanne's got a ton of video games. I saw them in the library. Man, I could spend the whole night messing with those."

Amy had to use the ladder to get out of the pool. "Louanne told me she'd help me make cookies sometime. My mommy used to do that."

Both youngsters stood dripping water onto the concrete. Their youthful blue eyes pleaded for Nesrin's approval.

"But, Amy, what about your kitty? Won't Sushan be lonely without you?"

Indecisive, Amy scrunched her face into a thoughtful expression. Then her eyes widened and she smiled. "Sushan can visit her brothers and sisters in the barn till I get back."

"The children do not even have their sleeping garments with them," Nesrin protested weakly, still seeking an excuse not to leave the children.

"That's no problem, honey. I got all kinds of pajamas around here for my grandkids. We'll find something that fits."

"But I'm not sure Parker and I should be alone." Until now, the children had provided some sort of a barrier to the urges they had both felt. With them gone...

Louanne wrapped her arm around Nesrin's shoulder. "Honey, there comes a time when a man and a woman don't need no youngsters around. I think for you and Parker, that time's about come."

"I'm afraid," Nesrin admitted. Her stomach did a little flip-flop, or maybe it was her heart turning over.

"Shucks, honey, all us girls get a little nervous now and again. Parker ain't gonna bite. You'll see."

Temptation was a terrible thing, indecision even worse. Nesrin was not sure she understood all the implications of what Louanne had said. But some urge she could not quite identify insisted she agree.

"Well . . . if you think Parker will not mind the children staying."

Both children cheered and wrapped their arms around Nesrin in a soaking-wet hug. She laughed. She was not at all sure she should have agreed to being alone with Parker. But how could anyone resist two such adorable children, whom she had also grown to love?

Chapter Seven

She was going to submit to Parker Dunlap.

The possibility terrified Nesrin.

With all of her powers, she fought against the inevitability of such a reckless act. She railed at the unutterable torment of discovering the one thing her heart most desired, and knowing if she accepted such a gift she would be condemning herself back into darkness—dreadful, lonely blackness that never ended, from which not even Parker would have the power to release her.

Yet she so desperately wanted to be touched by Parker's special magic, even if she would be allowed that pleasure only once.

Foolish woman.

She remembered every word Rasheyd had used to curse her into the darkness of the lamp. They had echoed starkly in her mind for centuries in an ancient dialect so foreign the harsh syllables sounded unfamiliar to her own ears.

Her vision blurred. Her trembling fingers worked without conscious thought, tearing bits of lettuce for their dinner salad into smaller and smaller pieces.

Standing nearby, Parker opened the refrigerator and retrieved a beer. He popped the lid.

Nesrin flinched, and ripped the lettuce leaf into even more minuscule portions.

"You sure the kids are going to be all right with Louanne?" he asked. "Kevin can be a handful. I wouldn't want him to drive her crazy."

"She seemed happy to have them stay with her." Nesrin was far more likely to face insanity than Louanne. Her thoughts tumbled and jumbled through her head in a bewildering tangle, like a twisted skein of silken threads in hopeless disarray.

"I admit it's nice with just the two of us for a change. Cozy."

"Yes." She would have chosen a different word to describe how it felt. *Intimate* came to mind. Fraught with possibilities. And danger.

"Guess we have to thank Louanne for looking after them."

"She is a very good friend." A friend who was generous with her advice.

Though Nesrin did not dare look directly at Parker, she was acutely aware of him leaning casually against the kitchen counter, one booted foot crossed over the other. He appeared relaxed, but she wondered if he was disguising a keen alertness, like a swift predator feigns lazy disinterest until, with a final burst of speed, he captures his quarry.

"The men who came to the house?" she asked, her fingers working rapidly to shred another piece of lettuce. "You are sure they will not return?"

"Not unless they get a court order, which doesn't strike me as very likely. You don't have to worry about them anymore."

That was fortunate, because Nesrin had a great many other matters on her mind at the moment.

"Nesrin..."

Her hands stilled at the question in his tone. Would he ask her to submit now, when she had not yet won her battle against temptation?

"Are you planning to feed another army?"

Lifting her gaze, she stared at him innocently. "Army?"

The corners of his mouth twitched into a smile. "It looks to me like you've shredded enough lettuce for at least a brigade."

"Oh, my..." A mountain of lettuce filled the serving bowl. Flustered, she snatched up a carrot from the counter and began slicing it into paper-thin circles. "Louanne says fresh vegetables are good for us."

"Lots of vitamins." His mocking voice teased across her nerve endings like the shivery caress of a summer breeze. Or, she imagined, like the skilled hands of a lover.

She chopped at the carrot with rapid, agitated strokes. Her heart echoed the same erratic beat. "She says we must eat three servings of vegetables each day, and several more of grains. Meat, we should have only—'' The blade came down on her finger.

With a soft cry, she sucked in a breath.

''What's wrong?''

A slender red ribbon of blood marked the tip of her finger. ''It is nothing.'' There was little pain, still she could not halt the tears that filled her eyes. If he asked her to submit, where would she find the courage to say no? Or the bravery to say yes?

He took her hand. Turning on the water, he placed her finger beneath the cold liquid stream. The cut stung, but in no way did the feeling dim the sensation of Parker's closeness, the sense of his broad chest so near, his height, and his quietly radiating power that had nothing to do with physical strength but came from somewhere inside.

''You need to be more careful.''

''A silly accident.''

As he rinsed the blood from her finger, she and Parker seemed connected—as a bee to pollen, a flower to the sun, night to day. Separate but inseparable, needing each other, and in their natural contrast making one the more precious because of the other.

Outside, the clouds continued to build against the mountains, and the sound of thunder rumbled in the distance. Within Nesrin she felt the same turmoil.

Parker shut off the water and dried Nesrin's hand with a paper towel. She looked as edgy as a filly who was about to come into heat—interested but not quite ready. He had in mind to encourage the next step in the process. Without rushing her, of course. Or frightening her as he had in town earlier in the day.

Slow and easy, he told himself, hoping his body would obey his command.

He soothed back a few strands of her dark hair from her face, thinking he'd like to see her hair loose, spreading like a fan across his pillow. Better yet, he'd like to feel the long, silken strands draped across his chest.

Slowly, with the tip of his finger, he explored the delicate swirls of her ear, knowing there were other, more intimate places he would like to investigate with equal ease.

Her eyes questioned him—or maybe she was questioning her own responses. He couldn't be sure which. But he noted how her eyes had darkened from a warm, sultry brown to almost black, and how her chest rose and fell with accelerated breathing. When her tongue darted out to moisten her lips, fierce need shot through Parker. He ached for her. Painfully. He wanted to take her right here in front of the kitchen sink, lift her off her feet, prop her on the tile counter so she could wrap her legs around him, and impale himself in her tight warmth. Just as earlier he'd wanted to take her on the hood of his car.

He'd never felt like that about any other woman. Now, twice in one day...

His head began to buzz with the urgency of his need, the heated images, and it took him an instant to realize the sound he heard was the damn oven timer going off.

He swore under his breath. His hunger had nothing to do with whatever the hell was cooking.

Nesrin slipped from Parker's grasp. He was weaving a spell around her that drained her will and left her feeling breathless. He shouldn't touch her like that. So gently. As though she had already agreed to submit to him.

"The chicken must be ready," she said as she turned away, her voice reed thin and lacking determination.

"Great."

"It is late." Almost dark, she realized, the storm bringing night to the mountains early. "You must be hungry."

"Very."

He was still standing close, forcing her to move around him as she found plates and served up pieces of chicken as she had been taught. Potatoes, too. The overly full salad bowl she placed on the table.

"A big man like you needs much nourishment in order to be strong," she said.

"Food's not the only thing a man can need."

The same could be said for a woman. She had never been so aware of her other needs, cravings that were making themselves known, and rivaled food and water in their importance. Even the air she breathed, filled with Parker's musky scent, seemed suddenly of lesser relevance than satisfying the velvet heat of her forbidden desire.

She closed her eyes and, with a shudder, forced herself to remember the impenetrable darkness she had endured for so many centuries. She would pay a high price to appease the dictates of her newly aroused appetite.

Without tasting a single bite, she ate her meal. She thought she and Parker spoke of ordinary things, of the horses he was training, of Kevin and Amy, and how they were adjusting to their new home. But she couldn't be sure. His words blurred, like her vision, obscured by the veil of her fears.

The blessed light shone brightly from the ceiling, filling the dark corners of the kitchen, casting appealing shadows across Parker's face. Outside, the storm rumbled closer. Temptation vibrated through her body with the low-throated sound of thunder.

If only she could cast a spell strong enough to protect herself from Rasheyd. But she had not the power.

Hastily she cleaned the dinner dishes.

"Nesrin, is there something wrong?" He snared her by the arm, his fingers long and tan and strong as they sank gently into her flesh.

"No." *Oh, yes,* her heart cried. Life was too unfair, and living it too precious. "I am tired. I thought I would go to bed early."

"I thought maybe we could…" His voice trailed off, low and suggestive.

She forced a refusal from her throat.

"No. I have to—"

Bolting from the kitchen, she fled through the house and up the staircase to her room. She had not submitted, she thought with relief flooding through her. She had not risked eternal darkness—and though she cursed the oracles, she hated herself for the weakness of her spirit. If Parker was the man she loved—and she did not for a moment question that knowledge—then she should trust that his powers far exceeded those of an evil wizard. But if she was wrong...

She shed her clothing, dropping bits and pieces onto the floor helter-skelter, and slipped into her sleeping garment. The fabric fell sensuously along the length of her body, stroking her flesh in the same way she wanted to feel Parker's hands moving over her.

In a transparent lie, she assured herself these needs that so consumed her would pass come the dawn.

The pace of the storm quickened.

Lightning left its jagged mark in the night sky, and thunder followed almost before the image faded.

The bed light flickered.

She pulled back the blankets. If she slept, temptation would not—

The room went dark.

Instantly and completely, everything was black. Empty. A void filled with only the crashing sound of thunder, and Nesrin's cry of terror.

She raced out of the room, into the darkened hallway and right into Parker's arms. He was warmth and strength, and she knew he was the light her soul had searched for during all those centuries of loneliness.

"Don't be afraid, sweetheart." He wrapped his arms securely around her. "It's only the storm."

"Darkness has always frightened me." She trembled against him.

"I'll get you some candles."

It was his light she needed, not a flame that quickly withered in the slightest breeze. "I am fine, now that you are holding me."

"If Rusty hadn't messed with the generator, I could get the power back on. As it is, we may be without juice for a while. I think the transformer may have taken a hit."

Nesrin realized Louanne was right. Love must surely be a talisman to any evil spell, however powerful. She need not fear. Parker, and her love for him, would protect her from eternal darkness.

She slid her hands up his chest and framed his unseen face between her palms—familiar features she needed no light to see. Evening whiskers roughened his jaw. Raising on tiptoe, she found his lips with hers. As they kissed, their bodies collided ever so lightly—soft breasts to unyielding chest.

He drew her closer. The sheer fabric of her gown brushed against the coarse denim of his jeans as they stood thigh to thigh. Heat spread from one to the other.

She sighed softly, opening to the gentle probe of his tongue. Like a parched desert traveler lost in the wilderness, his flavor refreshed her.

He groaned. "Nesrin, honey, if you keep this up I can't be responsible for what happens."

The need in his voice warmed and liquified Nesrin's insides. He too felt the magic that flowed between them—mystic magic older than time, yet as new as morning dew moistening secret petals with desire.

"This is a thing that is meant to be," she said in a whisper against his lips.

"You're sure, Nesrin? I have to know this is what you want."

"Yes." If need be, this was the memory she wanted to carry with her back into the darkness.

Parker scooped her into his arms. He didn't need a light to know she was the sexiest woman he'd ever seen. Or to admit he'd never wanted a woman more than he wanted Nesrin. But he was greedy. He wanted to see her, wanted to watch her expression as they made love the first time. He wanted to savor every instant of her passion.

In a few quick strides, he carried her down the hallway and into his bedroom. Slowly, almost reluctantly, he settled her on her feet, letting her slide down his body so that she could feel the hard evidence of his arousal.

She gasped softly.

Releasing her, he said, "There's a candle on the dresser."

He struck a match. The mirror reflected the flame's glow, as did Nesrin's dark eyes. His hand shook when he touched the match to the wick. Incredibly, his control was already teetering on the edge.

She reminded him of a dream. The filmy gown she wore made her appear insubstantial. But she was real. Hot and eager even in her innocence. The combination fired his imagination. His body throbbed with increasing desire. He vowed as he lifted the gown from her slender body that this would be no quick coming together. He would take care.

The candlelight gilded the soft curves and valleys of her body in a warm glow. He loosened the tie that held her hair back, and shifted the luxurious curtain over her shoulder, teasing himself as he hid one delicate breast from his view. Dipping his head, he kissed the breast he had left bared.

Her trembling response shuddered through him.

"You're lovely." His husky words were a mere whisper.

"I am glad I please you."

"Oh, yeah, you please me very much." So much it hurt.

He tugged his shirttail from his pants, and when his fingers went suddenly clumsy, she helped him undo the buttons. He would have been happy enough to rip the buttons off, but her untutored efforts were a sweet torture of denial.

With her palms, Nesrin eagerly explored the light furring of hair on Parker's chest. The curls were more silken than she had imagined, yet masculine in the way they roughened his skin. She found his nipples. They pebbled beneath her hands, much as her breasts were growing fuller at his touch. Fascinating. Erotic.

He lifted her again, placing her gently on his bed. Unclothed, skin against skin, they lay together, and the journey he led her on was more sensual with each new discovery. Nesrin was beyond fear, beyond reason. She responded to Parker's coaxing and his fiery kisses with such intense pleasure, her world contracted to a single focus. Parker. His hands. His lips. The talent of his tongue.

He laved her nipple and the heat of the velvet texture sent flames licking through her body more intense than the radiance of a desert sun. His hand spread across her belly, then his fingers dipped lower to that sensitive spot where she ached.

She arched against him. At the back of her throat, she made soft, wordless sounds. Hungry murmurs, like a woman starved for a sweet taste of the banquet he offered.

His tangy flavor intoxicated her senses. She was drunk on the forbidden need she now wanted to savor.

When she thought she could endure no more, he rose above her. She grabbed at his shoulders. She kneaded masculine flesh with her fingers, explored muscles and sinew, mapping the rugged landscape and committing every plain and valley to her memory.

"Please," she pleaded, though she could not yet fully understand what she sought. She knew that only release from this sweet torment would assuage the hunger of her soul.

"Go slow, Nesrin . . . I don't want to hurt you."

When he hesitated, when the pressure built to an intolerable level, she arched upward. The pain of his penetration, mixed with the explosive joy of release, slicing through her in dual prongs of happiness. Through all eternity she would remember this moment.

Nesrin's cry of pleasure catapulted Parker over the brink. Watching her in the throes of completion brought him more satisfaction than he had ever before experienced. His release, matched so closely with hers, stunned him with its ferocity. Shudder after shudder rippled through his body, and he felt Nesrin's answering response.

He had the oddest feeling they were floating high above a desert, drifting on a gentle breeze as easily as if they rode on a magic carpet. The air was filled with the dry scent of desert blooms. Above them, hawks dipped and soared through a blue sky.

Then slowly, gently, he settled back to earth, his fall cushioned by a thousand satin pillows.

Propped on his elbows, he waited for his breathing to ease, his heart to slow, and the strange images to slip into memory. Ages passed, bringing with them a new-found lethargy. He was too heavy for Nesrin and knew it.

He rolled away, taking her with him. She rested her head on his chest. Satisfied beyond any previous experience, he brushed a kiss to her damp forehead. In the distance, the thunder marked the storm's passage across the Rockies. A lullaby.

He must have dozed.

He wasn't sure how long he slept. Seconds. Minutes. It was hard to tell.

Turning in search of Nesrin, to pull her back into his arms, he found her side of the bed empty.

He felt a strange sense of panic—irrational, he admitted, yet the feeling had the same power as a nightmare had to startle a person awake. Images of mud huts, hidden vaults beneath desert sands, and evil wizards came to him. Grotesque and frightening.

Still blurry with sleep, he tried to assure himself Nesrin couldn't have gone far. This was the twentieth century and he lived on a ranch in Colorado.

But where the hell was she?

Chapter Eight

The candle had burned out and he nearly knocked over the useless lamp trying to find his flashlight. Then he stubbed his damn toe.

Cursing under his breath, he wondered where Nesrin had gone. He wanted her back in his arms. Now.

He yanked on his jeans. The whole house was silent. No water running in the bathroom. No glow of candlelight coming from any of the upstairs bedrooms.

He paused at her bedroom door. Not a sound. No quiet breathing. No restless stirring on her bed beyond the open door.

She was simply gone.

Making his way downstairs, he worried that maybe he'd hurt her. He'd felt the barrier of her virginity. Since she had such an innocent quality about her, that hadn't really surprised him. Instead, he'd been filled with masculine pride that he had been her first lover.

But maybe, in spite of his vow to take things easy, he'd gone too fast. Scared her.

Relief washed over him when he spotted the glow of lights in the living room. Looking small and fragile and very vulnerable in her see-through nightgown, she sat curled up on the couch surrounded by a dozen flickering candles. A band tightened painfully around his chest. He fought the sensation. There was no reason to confuse terrific sex with an emotion he wasn't capable of giving.

"Nesrin..." He spoke softly so he wouldn't startle her.

She raised luminous eyes to him and he felt a new shifting and settling deep inside that had nothing to do with sex.

"It's late, sweetheart. Can you come back to bed now?" He wouldn't touch her, if that's what she wanted. Just keep her near to him. Safe.

"I do not want to sleep." Her tone was flat and lifeless.

Worried, Parker sat down on the couch next to her. "Why can't you sleep?" He'd been so drained, he couldn't possibly have stayed awake if he'd tried. For such a petite woman, she was a powerful package. He thought he had satisfied her, too.

"Because..." Her chin trembled and she began to shiver. She wrapped her arms around herself. "Because Rasheyd will be here soon. Then there will always be darkness for me."

"I told you neither of those two guys this afternoon was Rasheyd. It's going to be okay."

"No, you do not understand. It is part of the curse. He wanted to bed me and I refused." She shivered uncontrollably. "He swore if . . . if I ever submitted to another, he would search me out and send me back into the lamp forever. Oh, Parker—" Sobbing, she threw herself into his arms. "I do not want to go back into the lamp."

"You mean, you thought by us making love you'd have to—" God, he'd never known anyone courageous enough to make that kind of a sacrifice, however misguided her reasoning might be. *She* believed the curse was true. That made her one gutsy lady.

It didn't matter whether he believed her story or not, Parker had to find a way to ease her mind. He slid his fingers through the lush thickness of her hair. Kneading her scalp, he tipped her head back so he could look into her eyes. "Honey, you didn't *submit* to me, if that's what you're afraid of. What we did upstairs, we did as equal partners. We both gave pleasure, and took it in return."

She gazed at him quizzically. "Is that different than submitting?"

"Damn right it is." A lot different than the apparent rape this Rasheyd jerk had planned. "So you see, you don't have to worry about him anymore. He's gone forever."

She didn't look entirely convinced. "*Partners* does have a nice sound to it," she conceded. "Not at all like *submitting*."

"Nope."

"More like . . . love?"

He stood and pulled her to her feet. Her arms were covered with gooseflesh. He rubbed them. How could he explain a man who had never been taught about love, didn't know the meaning of the word? "Let's get back to bed before you catch a chill."

She came along easily enough, as though she were considering what he had told her. She even snuggled up to him once he got her into bed, her back curled up next to his chest. He could still smell the scent of sex in the air mixing with the erotic fragrance that was so uniquely Nesrin's. It made him ache for her even more powerfully than he had before.

"Parker," she said after they had lain spooned together for a while. "Could we be partners again?"

He smiled. "Sure. Whenever you want."

"Now, I think would be a good time."

"Honey, I don't think—"

She turned in his arms. "Even if you are wrong, and Rasheyd will soon seek me out, I do not think forever will last any longer if you and I have been partners more than once."

Her logic was unassailable. "Good point," he agreed.

"I fear, however, that last time you gave more pleasure than you received."

"I figured it was pretty equal." What wasn't quite fair was the way her hand had slipped down his stomach. He groaned. "You're a fast learner."

"I have an expert teacher."

Nesrin marveled that by giving Parker pleasure in this way, her enjoyment grew even greater. She cherished his soft groans that told her she pleased him, for his caresses gladdened both her heart and her body.

When Parker pulled her on top of him, Nesrin realized it was his way of easing the slight discomfort she felt between her thighs. She loved him all the more for his thoughtfulness.

With his finger he touched her where they were joined, circling slowly before he increased the pace. The feeling was so intense she felt as though she were racing up a mountain peak. When she crested the top, she found they were there together . . . tumbling through space and time as though they were one. She sobbed his name and clung to him, her body pulsating in the magical moment.

Finally, when her breathing slowed and her heart beat normally again, she surrendered herself to sleep in the comforting security of Parker's arms.

HIS CONSCIENCE BEGAN to bother him as the first streaks of gray lightened the eastern sky. The storm was gone, but the clouds from his past still cast a pall over the present.

He'd known from the beginning that Nesrin deserved more than he was capable of giving. But his hormones had been doing his thinking for him ever since she showed up on the ranch. Not only had he taken her virginity, but by making love to her without being honest first, he'd made unspoken promises he couldn't keep.

In the past few years, when his needs simply became too powerful for him to ignore, he'd had a relationship with a woman who knew up front there'd be no permanent commitment. He kept it simple.

He'd violated his own principles with Nesrin.

He hadn't been honest, and now he cursed himself for that significant oversight.

Like most women, she'd wake up with certain expectations. In particular, a fantasy called love.

His stomach knotted. When they'd been handing out the capacity for that specific emotion, he'd been missing from the line. *Just like his father.*

Truth was, he was on the edge of not even being able to provide a home for himself and the kids, forget about any deeper emotions. He sure as hell couldn't deal with a woman in his life right now. His job was saddle-breaking the mustangs, and keeping the general from getting custody of Amy and Kevin.

Carefully, so he wouldn't awaken Nesrin, he slipped out of bed and pulled on his clothes. Before he left the room he gave her a long, hungry look.

She lay curled on her side, both vulnerable and desirable. Her lips were slightly parted, and full, as though they had been well kissed. Her dark lashes formed delicate fans that emphasized her classic features—a slender nose, high cheekbones, a finely arched jaw. He remembered her soft sounds of pleasure when he'd kissed her at the juncture of neck and her shoulder. And the sultry scent that was so distinctly Nesrin's.

Gritting his teeth against the images, he pulled the sheet up to cover her bare shoulder, then left the room.

"EASY, LITTLE LADY. Nobody's going to hurt you. We're friends, you and me. Good friends."

Nesrin smiled as she walked toward the corral.

Parker had a mare on a lead, coaxing her, stroking her withers, calming her as he accustomed the animal to the feel of the blanket on her back. He moved with easy, masculine grace, confident of his ability to master the mare. His jeans were old and faded, his shirt the same. Mud caked his boots. But to Nesrin he was a more impressive sight than any sheikh wearing flowing robes, or whose fingers sported rings covered with precious gems.

Quietly admiring him as he worked, Nesrin rested her elbows on the top rail of the fence. Parker was a very gentle man. He had been patient with her. Tender. Loving, she thought, though he had not said the words.

She only wished he had not left her to wake up alone in his big bed. What if Rasheyd had appeared? She might not have had a chance for one last memory of Parker to take with her into the darkness.

A slight movement Nesrin made caught Parker's attention. His heated gaze warmed her from across the corral. Then his expression changed, darkened, and she felt chilled to the bone.

He brought the horse to her. The mare nuzzled Nesrin's hand seeking a treat, and she rubbed the animal's velvet nose.

"I am sorry I have nothing for you," she said. "Next time I will bring you an apple or a carrot."

"Nesrin, there's something I should have told you. Before last night."

Only once had she seen such bleakness in a man's eyes. A crippled beggar on the streets of her village had been dying. He knew the end was near and no one could help him.

The thought that Parker—so strong and powerful, so vital—could be feeling the same despair terrified Nesrin. An ache formed in her chest.

"A woman like you needs a man who can love her. I can't be that man."

His words swept over her like an icy breeze from the glaciers high in the mountains. The hopelessness of her love froze in that spot where there had once been warmth. Her powers had been inadequate to bring forth the magic she had hoped for.

Stubborn determination and pride lifted her chin. "Then we must not partner together again." For knowing Parker could not love her meant what they had shared was little different than submitting, an act that might have already been at the cost of her freedom.

"I thought you might feel that way." He stroked the mare between her ears. "But I had to tell you anyway. I didn't want there to be any misunderstanding between us."

"You are a most thoughtful man." Her pain made her tongue as sharp as a scimitar, but he was beyond noticing.

"The Dunlap men aren't capable of love, Nesrin. I'm sorry."

She turned away because she could no longer look into the barren depths of Parker's eyes without seeing her own joyless future. How could he say he was not capable of love when she saw evidence of that ability in everything he did?

It was only she that he could not love, and that bitter recognition echoed with buried memories from the past.

Parker watched her walk away, silently giving himself a good sound thrashing. "Congratulations, buddy. Now you rank right up there with a guy who would kick Amy's kitten. Or kidnap a seeing-eye dog."

He took off his hat and slammed it to the ground in frustration. "Damn," he muttered.

He'd had to be honest with Nesrin. It wasn't fair to have her hoping for things that couldn't come true. In the long run, that would be best.

BY AFTERNOON, the pain in Nesrin's chest became unbearable. She started at every sound, sure Rasheyd had come for her. Through the window she watched Parker mastering the wild mares one after the other, knowing that she would never again feel his confident touch.

Never in all the centuries she had endured in the lamp had she felt more alone than she did at this dark moment in time.

Seeking solitude of a gentler sort, she slipped out the back door. The children were with Rusty and did not need her care. Somewhere in the rugged hills that surrounded the ranch she would find solace.

Once away from the ranch, she gave free rein to the horse she had saddled. The hot sun dried her tears as they crept down her cheeks. She came upon a small group of stray cattle, their tails switching at flies as they chewed their cud, and she thought perhaps they belonged to Louanne. Grasslands dotted with summer-faded wildflowers gave way to a pine forest.

As the trees closed around her the temperature cooled. She recognized the sound of a fast-running stream, and turned her horse in that direction.

She was near the spot where she, Parker and the children had once picnicked, she realized. With a shimmer of green and silver, the stand of aspen trees drew her.

Halting the horse, she gazed at the stream. Remembering. What was it about her that made her so unlovable? she questioned.

Her mount nickered softly.

Nesrin glanced up.

There, standing no more than a stone's throw away was the magnificent mustang stallion, Lucifer.

"Have you lost those you love, too?" she whispered.

The mustang remained silent and unmoving.

Nesrin's mount shifted uneasily.

"Parker would be very pleased if you would return to the ranch with me," she told the stallion. In fact, if she could capture Lucifer it would please him so much that he might smile once again at Nesrin. It was even possible, she reasoned with desperate hope, that he would find it in his heart to love her.

She nudged her horse forward.

"Your harem is waiting for you at the ranch," she cajoled. "And Parker is a kind man who will not beat you. So that he can save his ranch, he needs you."

Approaching Lucifer cautiously, she allowed the stallion to sniff at her mare. "If you would make this sacrifice, I know your women will be most grateful."

Taking a deep breath, Nesrin slid from her mount onto Lucifer's back. He sidestepped away from the mare.

"Come now," she urged. She squeezed with her legs. "I will show you the way to the ranch."

Parker saw Nesrin riding the stallion toward the corral, the docile mare right behind them, and his jaw went slack. It took him a full minute before he had enough presence of mind to open the gate.

Nesrin grinned down at him with a smile that filled him with guilt. She'd risked her neck capturing Lucifer, and all Parker had done was make her miserable. He couldn't bear the thought that she might have been hurt.

"The stallion will help you pay the moneylenders?" she asked brightly.

He reached up to lift her from the horse. Her waist was so tiny he could span it with his hands. He ached to fully hold her in his arms again, but he wasn't going to take advantage of her twice. He was, after all, supposed to be an honorable man. Not that he always acted the part.

He let go of her as soon as her feet touched the ground. "That was a fool thing for you to do, trying to capture a wild stallion on your own."

Her eyes widened at his gruff tone. "I only thought to please you."

"Yeah, well, next time I want to round up some mustangs, I'll get Rusty and the boys to do it. That's what they get paid for."

She blinked, and he knew she was fighting tears. "Do you wish me to leave this place?"

Parker's stomach knotted. "God, no, Nesrin. I don't want you to go. I . . . the kids need you."

"But if Rasheyd comes for me—"

"I swear, I won't let Rasheyd or anybody else hurt you or take you away. And as long as I own this ranch, you've got a home here. Understand?"

For a long moment there was just the sound of milling horses, hooves scraping against stones, then Nesrin gave a quick nod and spun away.

Parker was left with only a trace of her sultry scent to remind him that he was a fool.

GROUND BEEF. Noodles wrapped in cellophane. A can of soup and some vegetables.

Nesrin stared at the casserole ingredients she had spread out on the kitchen counter. The meat needed to be browned, onions and celery chopped, and the noodles cooked. What did it matter if she cast one little spell? Even if it might go slightly awry. Her cooking skills would certainly not earn her Parker's love.

It had been two days since she had submitted—partnered with Parker. For Nesrin, every moment had been a torment of joy alternating with the bitter realization that he did not love her.

She lifted her chin. This was but a small spell she had in mind. Quite simple.

Closing her eyes, she pictured meat nicely browned, a knife fairly flying as it chopped onions and celery, and noodles boiling merrily on the stove. A little tomato sauce, some mushroom soup, a few spoonfuls of grated cheese, and garlic for seasoning.

The phone rang in the other room, disrupting her concentration at a critical moment.

With a fair amount of dread, she opened one eye.

Her spirits plummeted. "Oh, sour figs!" she groaned.

"Hey, Nesrin," Parker called from the living room.

She raced to the kitchen door to intercept him. "Yes," she answered rather breathlessly, all the while blocking his access to the kitchen.

"That was Rusty on the phone. He's had a flat about halfway back from Louanne's with the kids in the truck, and he doesn't have a spare."

"Then you must assist him."

"Yeah, but I don't like the idea of leaving you alone."

"I am fine, Parker, and I have dinner to fix." She also had a very large mess that needed to be cleaned up before anyone saw it.

"I don't know." With his fingers, he combed a wayward lock of his hair back into place. Nesrin wished she could have done that.

"You must go. The children will be getting hungry unless Louanne has already spoiled their appetite with too many treats."

"Well, okay. I guess I won't be gone long." His expression still troubled, he warned, "Lock the door after I'm gone."

Nodding, she smiled. She could only hope he would be gone long enough for her to rid the kitchen of mounds of chopped onions and celery, and buckets of soggy noodles. Just once she wished her spells would go as ordered.

Almost as soon as Parker had left, Nesrin was elbow deep in disposing of the evidence of her faulty spell. She sorted through the mess. Eventually she piled an appropriate amount of ingredients in a dish and slid it into the oven.

She sighed. This time no one would know of her ineptitude.

A noise from the front of the house caused Nesrin to lift her head. Surely Parker had not returned so quickly.

With an uneasy feeling stroking down her spine, she went into the living room. She had forgotten Parker's warning to lock the door. She'd been so engrossed . . .

Two men stood in the middle of the room, both of them wearing dark suits. One held the brass lamp in his hands.

She gasped.

The men turned. Instantly she recognized Rasheyd, a gaunt man with dark eyes and a curving mustache beneath a beak nose, reminding her of an evil bird of prey. A nightmare that had come alive.

"Who are you?" he asked.

The tremors started deep inside her. Rasheyd had found her at last. Except he seemed to be subtly different and much younger than she remembered.

"Nesrin," she admitted, puzzled. He was not nearly as frightening as the man who had cursed her. And he had not known her name.

The second man, shorter and more stout than the first, said, "I thought we had gotten rid of everyone."

"You thought wrong," Rasheyd said.

"But the flat tire was all arranged. I planned it that way."

Shocked that these men had wanted the house empty, Nesrin took a step back. "Parker sent someone and he will return in a minute. And he has three other men with him. Strong men with guns," she warned. The two strangers did not seem concerned. Clearly they knew she lied.

Her gaze slipped to the lamp, and to the man's thumb circled with a tattoo of a snake. Knots filled her stomach. If not the Rasheyd she remembered, one from the same clan and equally evil.

He tracked her as she retreated toward the kitchen. "Our presence here is no concern of yours, servant girl. We only seek this lamp—" his dark eyes lit with avarice "—and the emeralds and rubies it will lead us to."

Her hand flew to her mouth. He knew of Rasheyd's conjuring room buried in the depths of the desert! And the elephant tusks inlaid with jewels. How was that possible after all these years?

"What is this?" He eyed her suspiciously. "You know about the treasure?"

She shook her head. "I know nothing, effendi. I swear it."

He saw through her new lie. "You do know something, lying daughter of Satan. When my cousin's wife reported she had seen this sacred lamp told of in ancient legends being packed and shipped to America, I knew there would be others who would try to steal it from me. You are the one, are you not?"

"No, you are wrong," Nesrin protested. "I do not wish to steal the lamp."

"But you have been studying the inscriptions, have you not?" He backed her up against the wall. His breath smelled of mint and rotten teeth. "Have you learned their secrets?"

Biting her lip, she shook her head again. Fear pelted her. "I am but an ignorant woman who cannot read, master." That was only a slight prevarication. Few of the symbols were familiar to her.

"Amir, find some rope," Rasheyd ordered his associate, "We are going to take this *ignorant* woman with us and make her tell us what she knows." His gaze skimmed over her in blatant hostility filled with sexual innuendo. "Forcing her to share her secrets will be my privilege. There is always room for one more in my small harem."

"No!" Nesrin broke away from him, but Amir caught her before she could escape. She smelled his foul body odor, and fought as he gagged and tied her.

The last thing she saw was a black hood being pulled down over her face. She swallowed the scream that rose in her throat.

Then all was darkness.

A muffled voice said, "We must find a way to slow *Mister* Dunlap's pursuit of this lovely young woman."

"More than the flat tire on his employee's vehicle, which we had already arranged?"

"A more challenging diversion, I think."

"What did you have in mind?"

"I believe *Mister* Dunlap would find it far more important to pursue his herd of fine horses, if they were to get loose, than he would in following us."

The second man laughed in a way that made Nesrin cringe. She feared, for all she might want to deny it, that Parker might indeed value his horses more than her.

"MAN, HAVE YOU EVER SEEN a tire flatter than that?" Kevin asked rhetorically. "Like a pancake." He was trying to help Rusty and Buck heft the heavy tire away from the truck, but mostly he was in the way.

"It wasn't Kevin's fault, Uncle Parker. Honest he didn't do anything bad."

"I know, honey." Parker grinned at Amy. It was hard to tell which child was more protective of the other, just like he and Marge had been. "Sometimes flats just happen. Particularly when we're driving around on such rough roads."

Amy seemed satisfied her brother wasn't going to take the blame and ambled off to investigate an outcrop of rocks tinted red with iron.

Parker studied the flat a minute, then said to Pete, "That looks like a brand-new tire."

"Yep." Pete rolled the spare into place. "We bought it jest a month or so back."

Parker frowned. "Hope you got a guarantee." Idly, while the men replaced the tire, he fingered the stem on the flat. There was no sign of damage to the tire and one this new shouldn't go flat. At least, not without reason.

Prickles of awareness rose on the back of Parker's neck.

He wrenched off the stem cap. "Damn!" The stem core had been loosened, allowing for a slow leak. No way could that have happened accidentally. It was sabotage! Somebody had arranged to lure him away and leave the ranch deserted—except for Nesrin.

"Rusty! Where's the cell phone?" Parker was already into the truck cab, searching for the instrument used by the hands to keep in touch when they were out working the fence line. He found it and dialed.

The phone rang. Once. Twice. He knew in his gut no one was going to answer, and still he waited through five rings.

"Get back to the ranch as fast as you can," Parker ordered. "Nesrin's in trouble."

He raced to his own truck. Wheeling it into a sharp U-turn, he rocketed back along the rutted trail he'd just followed. Who the hell would want to sabotage Rusty's old truck? And get him away from the house?

He hadn't come up with any good answers by the time he got back to the ranch. But he sure as hell had a fair suspicion when he saw the corral gate was open and the horses gone, Lucifer included. He swore again. Somebody was out to get him—somebody who thought he could buy saddle-trained horses cheaper down the road if Parker couldn't make delivery on time.

He raced into the house and knew immediately the place was empty.

"Nesrin!" he called, heading for the kitchen where he'd last seen her.

She wasn't anywhere around, but there was a curl of smoke coming from the oven. He used a pot holder to retrieve the charbroiled casserole and place it on top of the stove. The place smelled of burning grease.

Then he searched the house. Top to bottom. And the barn and outbuildings. Then he went back inside.

When his hired hands showed up at the back door, the kids tumbling along behind them, and there was still no sign of Nesrin, Parker began having trouble keeping a panicky sensation under control. He was about to call Louanne when she arrived, too.

"Howdy, Parker. You gonna sit in on our dancin' lesson this afternoon?" Smiling with mock seduction, she rotated her bony hips.

"No, I was just looking for Nesrin. I thought maybe she'd gone over to your place." Which didn't make any sense, but still there was a possibility...

"She's not here?"

"Nope."

A half-dozen troubled faces turned to Parker. He flashed on Nesrin's fears of being sent back into the brass lamp, and his gut clenched. That was impossible. He didn't believe in curses or wizards or magic spells. But Rutherford Mildon, the horse trader, wouldn't have any reason to snatch Nesrin along with the horses. Unless she'd seen him in the act...

Whirling, Parker marched into the living room.

The damn lamp was gone! The spot on the mantel where the lamp belonged was empty.

No Nesrin. No lamp. No horses.

None of it made sense.

He struggled to keep his brain functioning in a logical way. Women didn't vanish into lamps, and lamps didn't just evaporate into thin air. Not in this century. Or any other, as far as he knew.

On the other hand, Rutherford was a shrewd horse trader. He probably lacked much in the way of ethics, but he wasn't a kidnapper, and certainly had no interest in an antique lamp.

Parker's head pounded and a muscle tightened in his jaw. His fingers flexed into fists. He had to make sense of the senseless.

The phone rang. He heard Kevin answer and hoped to God it was Nesrin calling. From somewhere. Anywhere.

"Uncle Parker, it's a colonel somebody for you."

In two strides he was at the phone.

"I finally came up with some information for you," Billingsly announced without preamble.

Better late than never. "What've you got?"

"The two gentlemen in question are Arab nationals from a rather obscure emirate. A friendly enough place but not one of the major players in the Middle East."

"Are they legit?"

"Nope. That's why it took my people a little longer than usual to get a lead on them. They're both traveling with phony passports."

Phony IDs, too, Parker thought, swearing under his breath. *Ministry of Antiquities,* my foot.

"So far we're sure of only one guy's actual name—Rasheyd Sha'lan."

Parker felt as if his stomach had ridden an elevator in a free-fall from about twenty floors up. The impossible couldn't be happening. He'd promised to keep Nesrin safe. My God, he berated himself, he'd left her alone when he'd promised . . .

"Are you serious? The guy's name is Rasheyd?" Parker asked.

"That's what I'm told. Sound familiar to you?"

It sure did, but he wasn't even going to try to explain about nine-hundred-year-old wizards and curses. In fact, he desperately wanted to deny there was any connection between Nesrin's phantom Rasheyd and the very contemporary guys who had shown up at his door. Instead, he said, "It's probably a common name over there."

"Maybe. At any rate, we almost didn't manage to figure out who they were. They're traveling by private jet. The plane took off an hour ago from a strip near you. They've filed a flight plan for a trip all the way back home."

Parker squeezed the phone tight. Nesrin was on board that plane. He knew it, dammit, he just knew it. And she wasn't inside any old lamp, either. If there was any sorcery going on, they would have flown home on a magic carpet. "You gotta stop 'em, Bill." Parker Dunlap never, *never* went back on his promises. Not one as important as this, protecting Nesrin.

Bill hesitated. "I don't think we can do that. International diplomacy—"

"Forget your damn diplomacy. They've got a friend of mine on board. They kidnapped her."

"A woman?"

"Yeah, a woman."

"U.S. citizen?"

"What does that matter?"

"I don't know, Parker. This is not a good time in our relationship with most of the Arab world. We're trying very hard not to rock the boat."

What did Parker care about rocking boats when Nesrin's life might be at stake? He might not be capable of loving her. But he *cared!* More than a little. And he had to get her back. This was one time when he damn well wasn't going to fail. "All right, buddy. If you can't stop 'em then I want you to get me into their country. Clandestinely."

"Hell, Parker, I can't do a thing like that. If you got caught we'd have an international incident on our hands."

"Bill, I'm asking you—I swear I'll never ask another favor of you. I *need* to get into that country. Now."

Parker could almost hear the colonel weighing his options. "You know if I do this it could cost me my career."

"Yeah." And if that happened, he'd have to deal with his guilt then. But not now. "It's important, man." He left unsaid the reminder that Bill's career would have abruptly and fatally ended three years ago if it hadn't been for Parker. He didn't have to. They both knew he was asking for the debt to be repaid. In full, if need be.

"I'll get back to you," Bill said.

"I'll be waiting."

When Parker hung up, the kitchen was filled with the taut silence of fear. Both kids were wide-eyed. The three hired hands seemed to have aged while they'd been listening to the phone call.

"Nesrin's in trouble?" Louanne asked, the first to break the spell.

"I think so," Parker admitted. Dammit, he'd told her to lock the door. Why hadn't she been more careful?

"Them two men that were askin' questions in town?"

"Probably."

"Uncle Parker...me and Amy were talking last night. We miss our folks a lot, but we decided..." Kevin looked down at the scuffed toe of his shoe. His laces were untied. As usual. "If we had to lose 'em and live with somebody else, we're glad it was you and Nesrin." He shrugged. "You're both real cool. And well..." He looped his arm around Amy. "Rusty's been telling us you might lose the ranch. If you need it, I've got some money you can have."

"You could sell my kitty," Amy offered. Her chin puckered. "Sushan's a real nice kitty and I bet some little girl would pay a whole bunch of money to have her."

"See, the most important thing," Kevin explained, "is that you bring Nesrin back."

Unfamiliar tears clogged Parker's throat so full he felt as though he'd swallowed an ostrich egg. "I'll bring her home safe, Kevin. I promise. And somehow we'll keep the ranch—without selling Sushan." Tugging Amy into his arms, Parker knew he shouldn't be making promises he couldn't guarantee, but he was damn well going to try his best. For all of them.

"See that you bring Nesrin home soon, young man." Brusquely Louanne wiped her eyes with the back of her hand. "I haven't finished up my belly dancing lessons and don't intend to miss out just 'cause you and her are gallivanting around somewheres. Meanwhile, these two youngsters kin stay with me."

"I'd be obliged," Parker said, realizing that within Louanne's angular body she had a heart of gold and a huge capacity for love.

"You don't have to worry about the ranch, boss," Rusty said. "We'll track down them mustangs, 'n' saddle-break 'em, too. In plenty of time to meet ol' Rutherford's contract."

Parker hoped it wouldn't be at the expense of too many broken bones on the part of his hired hands. In that case, the cost would be too high.

He'd find some other way to save the ranch. *And* losing the kids to his father.

He wished there was somewhere else he could get the money. But for now it looked as if he'd claimed the last favor anyone owed him.

At the moment, however, he didn't have time to give his personal problems any more thought, or his dreams for the ranch. His priorities were clear. He had to get himself to an obscure Arab country, find Nesrin and get her back home again—all without getting caught. It wasn't likely to be an easy assignment. Particularly considering Nesrin didn't have a passport.

Chapter Nine

He hadn't cast a single spell since he had kidnapped her. No doves had appeared in a puff of smoke; no balls had danced on an invisible string.

And Nesrin had not been cast back into the lamp.

She thought *this* Rasheyd must indeed be the weakest wizard in all the land, a poor likeness of the distant ancestor Nesrin had feared. Even *her* skills were of a far higher order than his.

Perhaps, over time, conjurers had lost their ability to tap into their magical powers, she mused.

She would have been all the more grateful for this turn of events had she not been Rasheyd's captive.

Blowing out a sigh, she examined the women's quarters where she was being held prisoner. Floral designs in bright shades of red and yellow decorated the floor tiles like an indoor garden. Couches and lounging pillows were covered with soft fabrics dyed in equally vivid colors. Beyond a sheer curtain that moved with the slightest breeze from the open door, there stood a real garden. Even in the heat of the day, trees provided cooling shade where captive parrots strutted and squawked on their elaborate perches.

Surrounding the garden and protecting the women's quarters were insurmountable walls, three times the height of an ordinary man. Within the house, guards patrolled the hallways.

Nesrin was trapped as surely as if she were back inside Rasheyd's lamp. Her eyes filled with tears. If only Parker was here, he would find a way to release her. Thoughts of him these past two days had been like a disturbing furrow plowing through her fears. She ached for his presence, yet knew what she really sought was his love. A futile hope.

The jangle of gold bracelets announced the arrival of Rasheyd's senior wife. Her nose was nearly as long as his, her dark eyes even more evil. Inside the confines of the women's quarters, away from the eyes of strangers, she wore a Western-style sundress that hung from her bony shoulders like a dress on a hanger.

"My husband grows impatient," Tuëma said. "You must tell him where the emeralds are."

"I have said I know nothing of the jewels he seeks." Actually, now that she was back in her homeland, she thought—given enough time and the ancient inscriptions on the lamp as guidance—she could find Rasheyd's buried room. Not that she could be sure the jewels would still be there, but the possibility was a tantalizing one.

A wistful smile tugged at the corners of her mouth as she thought how the emeralds and rubies would be more than enough to save Parker's ranch.

Tuëma's scowl deepened. "I warn you, you have no cause to smile. Rasheyd is planning to have you dance for his friends this evening. Afterward, he intends something special for you." She eyed Nesrin with little sympathy.

Nesrin's stomach roiled at the possibility. "Then help me escape, Tuëma. I will find a way to go back to America." To what? she wondered, remembering the bleak remoteness in Parker's eyes. "Surely you do not wish your husband to—"

"I want the jewels as much as he does. Perhaps more." Her narrow lips twisted into an ugly caricature of a smile. "If Rasheyd succeeds, he will see that I am well cared for."

"At what cost, Tuëma? Do you think so little of yourself that you would willingly share your husband with another woman?" Nesrin could not bear the thought of Parker partnering with another, even if he were to give her a sheikh's ransom in jewels.

Tuëma shrugged. "In that I have no choice." Narrowing her gaze, she jabbed Nesrin's chest with a long, bony finger. "Tell me now of the emeralds, or I shall do nothing to halt my husband's plans."

Nesrin felt sick at heart. She knew no matter what she said, Tuëma would do nothing to stop her husband. Unlike the women Nesrin remembered from her childhood, this woman was ruled by greed.

Only by denying any knowledge of the emeralds would Nesrin be able to escape the avarice of both husband and wife. She could but hope they would believe her ignorance and spare her the humiliation of submitting.

In spite of the midday heat, Nesrin shivered. Whatever happened, in her heart she would remember only the joy she had found in Parker's arms when she had still dreamed he could love her.

IF A MAN KNEW WHERE he was going he'd be able to make his way through the maze of the town's streets blindfolded. Every alley had a different scent—sawed pine dust where the carpenters worked, oil and grease an aromatic backdrop for automobile repair shops, all of which gave way on adjoining streets to coriander, turmeric, and the acrid scent of chickens, both living and dead.

Unfortunately, Parker didn't quite know where he was going.

He'd been in this small desert country for two days. Using generous bribes, and a fair amount of arm-twisting, he had finally gotten an address of sorts for Rasheyd. Not that the houses had anything as simple as a number posted to distinguish one from the other. It turned out the guy was a minor sheikh, and had a reputation for acting like a school-yard bully.

He'd also been informed a big party was scheduled for that evening at Rasheyd's, one where a new dancing girl would be on display. Nesrin, he was sure. And from the smug way the informant had told him, Parker guessed she would be in serious trouble if he didn't get her out of there before the evening was over.

He wished he'd had more time to plan her escape.

Decked out in the local native costume of a flowing white robe and a turban wrapped around his head, Parker strolled along trying to look as if he belonged. There were no streetlights in this part of town. Typical of a country being dragged reluctantly into the *fifteenth* century, only an occasional smoky torch cast light into the darkness.

From the outside, the houses looked pretty much alike—whitewashed walls with the only entrances heavy wooden doors.

He spotted a taxi pulling up to one of the gates. Three robed men, their fingers weighted down with flashy diamond rings, got out of the car. A servant opened the door to the party goers, and the sharp wail of an ancient flute spilled out from somewhere inside.

Concluding he'd found the right house, Parker crept past the taxi and fell into step behind the three invited guests. With the studied disdain that seemed to mark the wealthy in this small sheikhdom, he ignored the servant.

A moment later he was inside the house. He took up a position at the back of a crowd of maybe twenty men, all of them dressed exactly as he was. Servants mingled among them, offering coffee as black as diesel oil, sweetbread and fruit. The smell of lamp oil and hashish hung thickly in the room.

At some unseen cue the guests quieted.

The flute took up a new tune, subtly erotic and blatantly sensual. Castanets fluttered rhythmically.

Parker sighed in appreciation along with every other male in the place when Nesrin appeared. She moved with incredible grace. Her dancing veils swayed and tantalized, her undulating body suggesting every pleasure a man could imagine.

Trouble was, Nesrin's eyes were filled with fear.

This was no ordinary dance, he realized. She was scared to death of these men. Probably with good reason.

Parker broke out in a cold sweat.

He had to get Nesrin out of here.

Standing by the door he'd just come in were two hulking guards with scimitars that looked as though they had come right out of the *Arabian Nights*. Parker wasn't eager to run that gauntlet with Nesrin in tow.

The only other exit was through a rear garden and over a wall that looked to be about twenty feet high. Taking a mental inventory of the assault gear he had hidden beneath his robe, he figured going over that wall was their best chance.

He edged around to the far side of the room. No one noticed him. Every eye was on Nesrin as the flickering torchlight cast arousing shadows across her flesh sheened with sweat.

When outnumbered, the military theorists argued, diversion is the key. Parker figured twenty-something to one weren't bad odds, given his background in Special Forces, but he'd better go with the experts. This was just like a training exercise, he told himself. He'd traveled halfway around the world to rescue Nesrin because that's what a man was supposed to do.

There was no deeper meaning, no hidden emotion that had his adrenaline pumping a little harder than it should. He was simply doing his duty to a woman who had sought his protection.

So Parker did what he'd been trained to do. He tamped down any trace of emotion that managed to struggle to the surface. He wasn't capable of love anyway, he reminded himself.

Cautiously he lifted a torch from a wall holder. There were plenty of flammable materials around. Couches. Pillows. And the flowing robes the men wore. He ventured a guess nobody in this country had heard about fire-retardant fabrics.

He put the torch down close to a couch where a couple of guys were sitting, both of them so engrossed in Nesrin's performance their tongues were practically hanging out of their mouths. They were about to get a rude awakening. He rather wished he could stick around to punch out their lights just on general principle, but Nesrin's safety came first.

He worked his way toward her.

She missed a beat, and for an instant he thought she had spotted him. If she gave his presence away all bets would be off. And probably both of their heads, as well.

Nesrin regained her rhythm quickly. She'd been so glad and relieved to see Parker, she had almost cried his name aloud before she realized that would place him in grave danger. These men would be very angry if their evening's entertainment was disrupted. They might even become violent.

In her heart of hearts, Nesrin had doubted Parker would come for her. Certainly not so quickly. He must surely have been reluctant to leave his ranch when he was at imminent risk of losing it to the moneylenders.

She had no doubt he had the power to release her from her captivity, as he had from the lamp, but she did think he might welcome some assistance. And she had been forming her own desperate plan before his arrival.

She would cast just a small spell to divert everyone's attention and cloud their vision. Then she and Parker could claim the brass lamp that held so many secrets, and escape from Rasheyd.

Swaying with the music, she closed her eyes.

The first shout came from the far side of the room. Not where Parker had planted the torch, he realized, but where another torch was spewing sparks like a Fourth of July Roman candle. A second torch went off in the same way, quickly followed by a third. The room turned to pandemonium.

Parker didn't hesitate.

He raced to Nesrin. She flew into his arms.

"Oh, Parker...I am so glad you are here. Did you see what I did with the torches?"

"They're going off like it's a national holiday." He pulled her out into the garden, then retrieved a rope with a grappling hook from under his robe. "Did you get a hold of some flash powder and iron filings?" A clever stunt that he wished he had thought of himself.

"No, it was my spell. Though I did not mean—"

He tossed the grappling hook over the top of the garden wall, then tugged to pull the rope taut.

"What are you doing?" Nesrin asked.

"We're going over the wall. Climb onto my back and hang on tight." He squatted down.

"I cannot go."

His head snapped up. "What do you mean, you can't go? Those guys in there are going to have the fires out in a minute. Then they're going to be *very* upset."

"Yes, I know."

"We don't want to be around when they figure out we're to blame."

"I cannot leave without the lamp, Parker."

"Why the hell not?" He gazed at her incredulously. Didn't she realize what those men had in store for her?

"It holds the secret—"

The chaos inside had simmered into a controlled rage. Orders were being given. Loud and angry.

"We can't go back in there, Nesrin. We either go over the wall in one heck of a hurry, or we're trapped right here."

She eyed the top of the wall where the rope dangled, then her gaze darted around the garden. "We'll hide."

"Nesrin, no..." But she was already running across the garden into the deepest shadows.

She halted in front of a woven basket the size of the world's largest laundry hamper. "Get inside," she ordered. "They will think we have gone over the wall and will pursue us. When they have all left we will find the lamp."

Parker sputtered his objection. Anybody who'd ever seen a B movie would know to look inside that damn basket. But it was past time for arguing. The goons with the scimitars had just shown up in the garden, and Nesrin had already disappeared into the basket, her flowing skirts vanishing out of sight.

Parker pulled his sheathed bayonet from his boot. If they lifted the lid, they'd get one hell of a big surprise.

He'd overestimated the size of the basket. Cramped didn't begin to describe the situation.

"I had forgotten it would be so dark," Nesrin said. Her voice trembled.

"We'll be okay."

With a grunt, he rearranged their positions so she was more or less sitting in his lap. She sucked in a quick breath. He suspected it was as much from nerves as from the fact they were squashed together and he didn't have any place to put his hands except in enticing locations. Delightfully interesting places if the situation had been different.

Hell, he'd gotten as aroused as every other man in the room while she danced. She was hot, seductive and provocative—an advanced class in erotica.

She also smelled of rich spices—frankincense and myrrh, he imagined. Inhaling deeply, he buried his face in the silken strands of her hair. God, he'd missed her.

His body clenched with wanting. He admonished himself. This was hardly the time to lose control.

With his legs beginning to cramp, he hoped the thugs in the garden would get bored pretty soon. There was a riot going on. Shouting and yelling. He didn't need to know the language to understand curses and translate the words of irate bosses blaming their apologetic subordinates.

"Thank you for coming," Nesrin whispered in his ear, her breath like a warm breeze that flows unseen across the desert.

"Shh. Don't talk." He didn't want to risk giving their position away.

"I was very afraid."

"We'll be okay. Just keep quiet."

"Are the children all right?"

"They're with Louanne." A man of action, Parker figured the best way to silence her nervous chatter was with a kiss.

He found her parted lips and claimed them. The sweet warmth jolted him with memories—Nesrin lying naked on his bed, the spill of her dark hair across his pillow, the satisfied smile curling her lips. She had been gone only for a couple of days, yet he felt as though it had been an eternity.

But he didn't have time to dwell on what he'd like to be doing right now instead of being crammed inside a laundry basket. Or on the pleasures he would have to forego because he'd been a damn fool and told her the truth.

He kissed her until the ruckus in the garden grew quiet.

Drawing a deep breath to steady himself, he cautiously lifted the lid of the basket. Nobody in sight. Amazingly, Nesrin's idea of hiding had worked. So far.

"Let's go." He hefted her out of the basket and quickly followed suit.

"The lamp is in Rasheyd's private quarters."

"We don't have time to mess with that now. The guards will figure out in a minute that we didn't go over the wall."

"The lamp will lead us to the jewels."

"What jewels?"

"The ones I saw when the original Rasheyd condemned me into the lamp." She slipped away and hurried through the corridors.

Damn, she was still obsessing about being a genie. Hadn't she figured out yet that magic didn't exist? Not hers or anyone else's. Whatever she had experienced was a trick, nothing more than sleight of hand, just like torches turned into Roman candles by adding flash powder and a few metal filings to the flames. No supernatural forces working there.

When she found the lamp, she hugged it to her and smiled up at him. She was the most stubborn woman he'd ever known, and the most beautiful.

He took her hand. ''Now! No more excuses. We're getting out of here.'' Assuming they could get safely away from Rasheyd's house, getting out of the country was still going to be quite a trick.

As they made their way toward the front of the house, Parker heard voices. He shoved Nesrin into a shadowy alcove and held his breath. Two guys in white robes wandered by, talking excitedly. He waited till they were out of sight, then tugged Nesrin at a run toward the door.

They made it to the street before someone spotted them and shouted the alarm.

There were few people on the streets and even fewer places to hide. Parker and Nesrin raced past the closed shops of silversmiths, and down an alley that smelled of turpentine. Heavy footsteps pursued them.

A car turned into the alley, its headlights blinding, and Parker ducked down an even smaller passageway, dragging Nesrin along behind him. They nearly collided with an old man who was hobbling along with a walking stick.

''Alms for the poor?'' the old man asked, his hand extended.

Parker waved him out of the way.

''Parker! You have to give the man a coin.'' Nesrin dug in her heels. ''He asked very nicely.''

''Don't you remember what happened the last time you made me give money to some bum? He broke into my house.''

"That was in *your* country. Here our beggars are honorable men."

Parker rolled his eyes. There wasn't time to argue, particularly when he knew damn well he'd lose. The approaching voices were getting louder. And closer.

He fumbled under his robes, found his pocket and came up with a little loose change.

"May Allah bless your kindness," the old man said.

"I'll be happy if I can just get us away from those goons with the swords," Parker mumbled as he pulled Nesrin farther into the narrow passageway.

It was like running through a maze with no idea of the way out. The place was unmapped and unposted, traversed more by instinct than any real sense of direction.

"Parker, please..."

At Nesrin's breathless plea, Parker halted and gathered her into his arms. His heart was beating uncomfortably fast, and hers was fluttering like a hummingbird. He couldn't go on dragging her through an unfamiliar labyrinth of alleys and streets. There had to be somewhere they could hide out, but he'd had no time to arrange for a safe house.

For now, the pursuing voices seemed a little more distant. Maybe they'd taken enough twists and turns to lose them.

Just as they had both managed to catch their breath, torches appeared at the end of the alley where they were hiding.

"We have to go back the way we came," he said.

They turned and fled, through air redolent with spices and pine, and finally sharp with turpentine again. They were right back where they had started from, Parker realized in dismay.

"Alms for the poor." The old man was there again, hand extended.

"I gave at the office," Parker said grimly. He looked over his shoulder. They weren't going to get away unless he was willing to create a serious international incident. He hated to do that to his buddy in Washington. In another minute, though, he wouldn't have much choice.

"This way, effendi."

"What?"

The old man shoved open a door that had been nearly invisible in the darkness. "For your kindness, my family and I would be happy to share our simple home with you. Until the sheikh's men no longer have interest in your whereabouts."

Nesrin grinned up at Parker with an unspoken "I told you so."

He didn't need any more persuading.

Bending, Nesrin slipped into the safety of the beggar's hovel. A piece of her skirt caught on a jagged splinter of the doorjamb. She tugged it loose, ripping the material.

Three surprised faces looked up at the new arrivals, the beggar's aging wife and two youngsters who looked to be their grandchildren. They were all sitting around a small cook fire. Nesrin returned their hesitant smiles.

As grateful as she was to be safe in these cramped quarters that reeked of cooking oil, and as weary as she was from running pell-mell through back alleys and dark passageways, she felt discouraged about Parker. He had come to rescue her—for which she was over-joyed—yet he could not believe she was a genie. It was almost as demoralizing as her father's embarrassment over her lack of skills. Granted, her powers still had a tendency to go awry. She had only intended a curtain of smoke to blind Rasheyd's men, not a fountain of shim-mering sparks. Though the fireworks had been quite impressive, she conceded proudly.

The beggar gestured for them to be seated on a pile of rags, which Nesrin took to be the communal bed.

"I am Abdel," he said. "My family and I welcome you, effendi. What little we have, we will happily share with you."

"We appreciate you letting us hide out here," Parker said. "I confess, I'm a little surprised that you, ah, speak English so well."

Abdel smiled indulgently. "When I was a young man I worked in an English-speaking household but that was many years ago." He raised his shoulders in a fatalistic shrug. "Would you care for tea? It is not of the highest quality, but my wife would be honored if you would accept this small token of our hospitality."

The old woman bobbed her head and quickly set a pot of water over the fire.

"What we really need, Abdel, is some help getting to the airport. I need to get Nesrin out of the country as quickly as possible. A phony passport would help, too. It's going to be tough getting past Immigration.''

"But we do not have the jewels yet," she objected.

Abdel's eyebrows rose in inquiry.

"We aren't going to hang around here any longer than we have to, Nesrin. It's too dangerous.''

"But, Parker, you do not understand. As long as Rasheyd believes I know where the jewels are, he will come after me again and again. Anywhere in the world. I will never be safe until I have found the emeralds and rubies, or he is convinced I have no more knowledge about them than he.''

"You really think you can find them?''

"I cannot be sure, of course. I have only my memory, and the few words of this inscription as clues.'' She rubbed her fingertips over the raised marks on the lamp. "In some ways this is a map.''

"Where, might I inquire," Abdel asked, "would you expect to discover these jewels you speak of?''

In her mind's eye, Nesrin saw the winding maze of streets of her village, lined with the low huts of mud and stone, that led to the tribal chief's palace. And buried deep beneath that building lay the wizard's evil conjuring room. Fear shivered through her.

"In the village of my birth," she said. "A place in the desert sands of the interior.''

Abdel nodded.

Parker looked skeptical. "We can't go running around on our own in a strange country. We don't have any transportation. No backup in case we get in trouble. I won't put you at that kind of risk, Nesrin."

"The risk is greater if we do nothing," she reminded him. Though returning to that buried room filled her with trepidation. What if the wizard—or his evil soul—still existed in that place.

"If I may make a suggestion…" Abdel handed them each a cup of aromatic tea liberally laced with sugar. "It is possible, shall we say, to *borrow* a vehicle suitable for desert travel. Assuming you have sufficient cash available, of course. With such transport you could easily reach your destination without the sheikh or his men being aware of your departure."

"I don't think Nesrin is exactly dressed for travel." Parker eyed her dancing costume. "In the daylight, they'll spot her in a minute. It's going to be tough enough just getting her to the airport."

"Among our people, the women go out in public fully covered. One woman looks much like the other when veiled and dressed in black. Except for their feet, of course." His amused smile revealed two missing teeth. "It was my wife's delicate feet that first attracted me to her."

The old woman giggled and covered her mouth with her hand.

"Please, Parker, we must try," Nesrin urged. "It is a good plan. Rasheyd will expect us to try to make our escape immediately. His men will be watching the airport. They will not expect us to flee to the interior."

Sipping the heavily sweetened tea, Parker realized Nesrin was right about Rasheyd having the airport watched. It might actually be easier to make their escape in a day or two, when his guards had grown careless, rather than try to leave the country immediately.

Staying within the confines of the city, however, posed additional risks. People talked, particularly if there was a chance for a reward. Word of their whereabouts would very likely get back to Rasheyd.

A trip across the desert might indeed be their best shot at escape. Not that Parker expected to find any missing jewels.

Those emeralds and rubies were as much fantasy as Nesrin's obsession with magic.

"Abdel, could you arrange for suitable clothing for Nesrin, and make arrangements for the vehicle you're talking about?" From under his robe, he pulled out his wallet.

Accepting the money Parker offered, the old man dipped his head. "It shall be done."

Chapter Ten

This fell into the category of a wild-goose chase.

Last night it had seemed perfectly logical to go racing off across the desert in search of a supposed treasure that had been buried for nine hundred years in a village that no longer existed. At least, as an excuse to get out of town long enough for Rasheyd's men to lose interest, it had seemed reasonable enough.

In the blistering heat of midday, Parker was having second thoughts. The old four-wheel-drive truck Abdel had *borrowed,* with a transmission that whined threateningly and brakes that were erratic at best, wasn't exactly a confidence builder, either. This was not a place Parker wanted to get stuck.

"Is it not beautiful?" Nesrin said.

She'd lowered the veil that had covered her face while they drove through town, but she was still garbed in a solid black shapeless robe. There was nothing feminine about the dress. Except Parker could imagine every one of her delectable curves. The pert shape of her small breasts. Her narrow waist. The curve of her thigh he'd slowly stroked as she lay in his arms that one night an eternity ago.

Wheeling to avoid a particularly deep rut in the almost nonexistent road, he forced himself to set aside provocative thoughts.

"You must be looking out a different windshield than I am," he responded. For him, only a bleak, monochrome desert stretched out to the shimmering horizon—much like his future lengthened into meaningless time when he thought of not having Nesrin in his arms. Yet how could he hope to hold her? His background, his limitations, condemned him to a lifetime as colorless as the bleak landscape he saw.

"Perhaps I am seeing my homeland through my memories," she conceded. "I once caravanned with my father and brothers through this area. It was a magnificent sight, camels walking four or five abreast, roaring and ruckling and spitting." She laughed with the lightness of fine crystal. "In spite of all that, they move with great dignity, you know."

"I guess I've never thought much about camels."

"It was springtime, I remember. We had had good rains that year and grass was plentiful. Everywhere there were baby chicks cheeping and chirping in their nests. The sky was filled with their parents snapping up insects to feed many hungry mouths. And there were so many wildflowers their scent filled the air."

"Sounds terrific." But it had to be a figment of Nesrin's imagination. Or something that happened when she was a kid—in *this* century. He simply couldn't accept she was nine hundred years old.

Whether she was or not didn't matter, he told himself sternly. He wasn't going to touch her again. He'd made that promise back in Colorado, and he'd meant it. Whatever her age, she was too damn trusting to be hooked up with a guy who wasn't capable of love. He'd seen his mother turn into a bitter woman because of that fatal mistake. His ex-wife hadn't fared much better, though Parker wasn't sure it was entirely his fault. He suspected both he and his wife had confused lust, and a similar history of being raised as military brats, with love. It definitely hadn't worked.

Parker wasn't about to put Nesrin at that kind of risk.

The old truck labored up a slow incline. Almost imperceptibly the character of the landscape changed. Monotonous beige sand gave way to rose-tinted rocks, and low-growing vegetation appeared. A buzzard feeding on carrion was startled into awkward flight. Even the dry heat seemed to ease a degree or two, making drawing a breath a little easier.

"We should be almost there." Nesrin nervously fingered the inscription on the lamp. She was coming home. Her chest was tight with anticipation. Over the next rise, or perhaps the one after that, would be the village where she had grown up.

In her mind, she heard the children of the village playing in the streets, watched as the shepherds gathered their flocks, felt a spring breeze caress her cheeks with fragrant warmth. She remembered the taste of cool well water freshly drawn. In some halfhearted way she tried to prepare herself for the changes that must have taken place. But in her soul, she simply wanted to go home.

The truck drew to a halt.

"What is wrong?" she asked. "Why did you stop?"

"According to the map Abdel gave us, and your instructions, we're here."

She shook her head. "That is not possible. There is nothing...."

Her gaze slid past the windshield. She strained to see what her memory told her had once been there. The village was little more than a wind-picked carcass, a few lumps of dried mud and stone standing no higher than a man's waist. The knot of joyful anticipation turned rock hard and filled her throat.

Still clutching the lamp, she got out of the truck at Parker's urging.

Slowly she walked where there used to be streets. At each step, the lonely sound of her sandals mocked her memories. She had never been given a chance to say goodbye, not to friends or family. Her right to grow old in the village of her birth had been cruelly taken from her. With trembling fingers, she touched a low, weatherworn wall reverently, as if by doing so she could make the occupants come alive again—that the mud and stones heated by the sun would change to living flesh.

"This is where the blacksmith, Mishal, lived." Words of farewell formed thickly in her throat. "You can still see the stain of the coals where he worked iron into lances so our men could defend the village.''

She turned and looked across the street. "Nadya, the village midwife lived there. She was the one who helped my mother bring me into the world. They said the labor was long and hard...."

Nesrin's chin puckered. She lifted her eyes to Parker, knowing they were filled with the tears she had refused to shed years ago. "I tried so hard to be a good daughter. I knew my father blamed me for my mother's death. There was nothing I would not have done for him. Why did he..." A single tear spilled down her cheek.

"Look, Nesrin..." Warring instincts held Parker immobile. He wanted to hold her, to ease the memories that seemed so painful. But if he held her, he'd kiss her, sure as a thirsty man would drink, given a chance. And that would lead to indulging in other things that he had no business doing. "Let's get out of here. Maybe we can get this old truck as far as the border. Rasheyd won't be looking for us—"

"No, we must find the jewels."

"There isn't anything here. If there were any jewels around, don't you think the nomads would have found them by now?"

"They would not know where to look." She glanced at the lamp, her fingers skimming across the inscription as if she were reading braille.

Adding impatience to his high level of frustration, Parker speared his fingers though his hair. "Why are those damn emeralds so important to you? Is this about money?'' He supposed it wouldn't be the first time a woman had traveled halfway around the globe because of greed. His ex was certainly capable of that.

Anger flashed in her dark eyes. "It is about freedom, Parker. *My* freedom. The jewels mean nothing to me."

She whirled with the grace of a dancer, her black robe billowing, and marched away. She held her head high, her delicate shoulders thrown back. Parker had little choice but to follow her down what appeared to have once been a street.

The stillness was so intense, Parker detected minute sounds in the deserted village. The scurrying of a lizard heading for cover across the mounds of sand. The wind pressing on his eardrums. The sibilant sound of Nesrin's skirt, seductive and alluring as the hem flipped from side to side.

She stopped by a wall slightly higher than the rest of the ruins, and ran her fingertips across the rough stones. Her hand trembled.

"Here is where Rasheyd lived."

"Not recently," Parker said under his breath. The Rasheyd that Parker knew would have preferred somewhat more comfortable accommodations.

Ignoring Parker's comment, Nesrin glided through an opening in the low wall. She walked a few paces then turned to the left. The dry desert air fairly crackled, she was concentrating so hard.

Memories. A servant lazily swinging a pendulous fan through the air. Lounging couches covered in satin and decorated with brightly colored fringe. Flies humming around a half-eaten fig. The feel of cold tile beneath her bare feet. The desperate fear that had dried her throat and made her knees weak. The secret door that led down into the netherworld.

She saw it all, *felt* it all with the same stark terror that she had experienced when she had begged Rasheyd for mercy.

"We need a shovel." She spoke softly so as to not disturb the shimmering ghost images of the past.

"We can't dig up the whole desert," Parker warned.

"Beneath this rubble are the jewels." And the fears that had plagued Nesrin for nine hundred years. Today she would face them.

Parker produced a shovel from the back of the truck. When he returned to the ruins he found Nesrin had set the lamp aside. She was on her hands and knees scraping away the debris with an old piece of tile. If she wasn't so damn stubborn, she'd see there wasn't anything of value in this forsaken place.

"Let me do that," he ordered gruffly.

She stood and moved out of his way. "The secret door is near this spot."

"Try not to be too disappointed if we can't find it."

"This is the tile that decorated Rasheyd's floor. I remember it well."

Resigned to a long afternoon of hard work if he was going to satisfy Nesrin's whim, Parker slid the shovel into the debris. The sun beat down with fiery intensity on the back of his neck. Almost immediately a trickle of sweat edged along his spine. If he was going to avoid a sunstroke, he'd have to put the turban back on his head.

The third time he planted the shovel, it struck with a solid thud. Not rock or tile, he realized, but wood.

Frowning, he shoveled more of the dirt and stones out of the way. He told himself even old structures had wooden floors. But a rectangular shape was appearing. Big enough for a trapdoor.

He grunted. Sweat dripped down his face.

Remnants of color emerged, a swirl of gold on a background of white, paint worn by time and shifting sands.

"Yes," Nesrin whispered. "This is the place."

Her large, dark eyes seemed to focus on what lay beyond the heavy planks, and her face had gone pale. The tips of her black headdress fluttered on a dry breeze.

Possibilities Parker had never accepted threatened to dislodge reason.

He uncovered an iron handle embedded in the wood. He knelt. Gripping the handle, he tugged. The door didn't budge. Applying more effort, he pulled harder and felt his muscles strain. The darn thing weighed a ton.

Breathing hard, he sat back on his haunches. "We're going to need a crane. Or dynamite."

In a daze, Nesrin stepped back.

"He stood here," she said. Slowly, with her eyes closed, she raised her arms and held them out wide in supplication. "And commanded the door to open."

Parker heard the latch click. He grabbed the handle. This time the trapdoor lifted easily. A blast of cold, musty air escaped from the depths. "I'll be damned. A secret catch." Nesrin had known how to release it, he realized with a combination of shock and surprise.

Looking down into the shaft, he saw marble stairs leading into the darkness.

"I feel like we just opened King Tut's tomb," he said.

"No. It is Rasheyd's conjuring room. A place of evil."

"Yeah, well . . . I'll take a look." He unhooked a flashlight from his belt. "You stay here."

"I must go with you."

She looked too scared and unsteady on her feet to go anywhere, and the stairs were steep. But her chin was jutted out at that stubborn angle he'd grown to recognize.

"Okay. I'll go first. Stay close."

Dread gripped Nesrin, nearly paralyzing her. She placed her trembling hand on Parker's shoulder as they descended into the darkness. What if Rasheyd, the most powerful wizard of all time, waited for them in his conjuring room? Waited to condemn her back into the lamp.

Perspiration that had sheened her body dried in the cool air and she shivered. Would Parker have the power to protect her? The thought echoed hollowly in her mind in the same way their footsteps echoed in the marble chamber. Once again she heard the words of

Rasheyd's curse, words that had been etched forever in her memory.

The beam of Parker's flashlight flicked around the chamber as it widened into a room. When it landed on the pedestal, he sucked in a breath.

"My God..." He hurried forward and knelt to study the emeralds and rubies inlaid in the four ivory elephant tusks that made up the base of the pedestal. "No wonder Rasheyd was after these. They've gotta be worth a fortune."

Incredulity still filling his eyes, he said, "You knew. You knew these jewels were here."

"And all the while you doubted that I spoke the truth." In an astonishing moment of insight, Nesrin realized nothing she could have said would have made Parker believe her story until he saw the evidence for himself. Just as nothing she had ever done had gained her the love she sought from her father, the man who had wagered against her future. In some strange way, the realization lifted a terrible burden from her shoulders. For nine hundred years she had lied to herself about her father's love. No longer.

It was then she spotted a heap of tattered rags in the shadowed corner of the room.

Hesitantly she advanced on the pile of debris. Death was here, in the air she breathed. It tasted bitter on her tongue.

"Parker, shine your light in this direction."

From the shapeless form two eye sockets appeared. Skin dried to the texture of leather pulled taut across the sharp outline of cheekbones, the natural mummification in the absence of air and moisture preserving the body as carefully as if it were a museum piece. The jaw hung open in mute appeal. As the light swept the length of the rag-covered heap, Nesrin noted its fist clasped in futile anger against an unseen enemy. The dark outline of a snake circled the leatherlike skin of the dead man's thumb.

"Rasheyd." She spoke his name in whispered awe. Like her fears, the sound echoed hollowly.

Parker bent over to peer more closely at the skeleton. "Looks like he must have gotten trapped down here and couldn't get out."

"Perhaps the infidels attacked the village and Rasheyd hid here." She looked up the stairway toward the small square of sunlight. "For some reason, his powers failed him and he could no longer open the door. He died here...in the same darkness to which he had condemned me." The irony of Rasheyd's death conjured little sympathy for the evil man with Nesrin.

"This is the guy you've been afraid of all along?"

"My tormentor, yes. Foolish of me, wasn't it, to fear him when he was already turning to dust. He no longer had any power over me, yet I trembled in my heart in terror of him."

"When soldiers hit a beachhead they're more afraid of what their imagination has told them is going to happen than what's really there. It's not that unusual to be scared of ghosts. At night, when I was a kid, I used to be afraid of what was in my closet, and then in the morning I'd realize there wasn't anything there at all, except maybe the shadow of an old teddy bear sitting on the shelf.''

Turning to Parker, she said, ''We can go now.'' There was nothing here she needed, and at last she could put her fears of Rasheyd away. His curse no longer had power over her. She was free at last . . . to do what? she wondered.

''You don't mean for us to leave the jewels here, do you? My God, they're worth a fortune. You could buy half the state of Colorado with them.''

''I had forgotten.'' She blinked, trying to find herself in the shifting of time and place, of ancient curses and modern greed. ''Take them for your ranch, to pay your moneylenders.''

''Nesrin, I can't do that. You found them. They rightfully belong to you.''

''It is better that you and the children have them.'' Perhaps in some way the jewels would bring Parker the happiness he would not accept from her.

''Well, I sure don't want our modern-day Rasheyd to get his grimy hands on them.'' He tugged at the pedestal. Granted, the jewels would solve his financial problems and secure his dream of a horse ranch. But it wouldn't be fair to Nesrin to claim the treasure for himself. He'd simply have to count on his hired hands having finished breaking the horses in time to meet his contract deadline with Rutherford Mildon.

"I don't think this pedestal is going to come loose," Parker said, "and it's too heavy to carry anyway. I'll have to pry the stones out of their settings."

He began working on the stones one at a time. "If nothing else, these little babies are likely to be our ticket out of the country. There's still a chance Rasheyd and his men may catch up with us. We could use a little insurance." He held out his hand. "Give me the lamp. I'll put them in there."

Parker laboriously removed each of the precious gems and dropped them into the lamp. He could still hardly believe Nesrin knew how to find—and get into—this secret room. It would have taken an archaeologist years of painstaking research to find this place. Clearly she'd been here before.

He didn't even want to consider the remote possibility that the rest of her story was equally true. He couldn't quite handle thinking of her as a genie. What man would be comfortable with a woman who popped out of lamps and cast spells with the sweep of a see-through veil?

When they emerged from the cellar, night had fallen as only it could in the desert. Quick and complete in an instant, darkness like velvet shrouded the landscape.

Parker leaned the shovel against the side of the truck. "Looks like we're stuck here for the night. Without a decent road to follow back to town, we'd either get lost in the dark or break an axle."

"Abdel provided us with supplies, did he not?"

"Yeah. There're some rations and a couple of blankets."

"Then we shall stay. I will find fuel for a fire."

Parker hadn't intended to be stranded in the middle of the desert with Nesrin. In spite of the vast empty landscape beyond the truck, the darkness provided a unique sense of intimacy. The rest of the world could have vanished for all it mattered. There were simply two people. Alone.

And one of them had a libido that kept cranking along in high gear no matter what Parker told himself.

He tried counting to a hundred. Instead of being distracted, he found himself watching her robed shadow moving like a woman of mystery around the campsite they'd set up. When she bent over the small fire she'd started, her long hair shifted forward like a curtain. Then she lifted and tilted her head to swing the long strands back out of the way. He wanted to learn all of her most private secrets, memorize the nuances of her most subtle mannerisms.

There sure wasn't any place to take a cold shower, so he splashed some lukewarm canteen water in his face. He remembered the unique musky flavor of her skin, and her warmth. He took a big drink of water. In no way did it slake his thirst.

Abdel had been right about a woman's feet. If that was all you could see, they became strangely intriguing. Nesrin's toes were beautifully shaped, long and slender, and the high arch of her foot made him think of how he wanted her arching up to his body. The entwining slender gold chains around her ankle drew his attention with a promise that her calf would be equally well shaped.

What he wouldn't give to be able to kiss that artistically formed ankle right now and hold her delicate foot in his hand. Not tickling, but massaging her tenderly. He'd like to place a moist kiss in the most sensitive spot he could find. His tongue would explore new territory until...

Damned if he wasn't tempted to get into the truck and drive them back to town as best he could, forgetting about the risk of broken axles. At least driving would keep his mind occupied with something other than thoughts of burying himself deep inside Nesrin's sweet, velvety warmth.

He gritted his teeth. He wasn't going to lay a hand on her. For her sake, he could deny the wanting that kept gnawing at his gut. Self-control. Discipline. That's what he'd been taught.

The lesson had never been more difficult.

They ate dried meat that tasted like cardboard, nibbled on dates, and washed it all down with a weak tea sweetened with sugar. The tiny flame from the camp fire cast a flickering glow across Nesrin's classic features, first highlighting her slender nose before moving on to draw attention to her cheekbones, a determined jaw and, finally, her full, sensuous lips.

In the distance, a wolf howled at the rising moon. The eerie sound undulated across the desert.

"Sounds like we're not entirely alone," he said.

Nesrin shivered, remembering the sound from her youth. "When I was young, there were times when the wolves became too bold, stealing into the village to snatch babies from their mother's arms, or to attack old women when they carried water from the well. The men would hunt them down on horseback and slaughter them with their lances."

"Sounds like some of them got away."

"They are a very cunning breed." Perhaps more shrewd than the villagers had been, for they were gone and the wolves remained.

Made restless by the night sounds, she stood. "It was on nights like this that I danced for my father's friends. They smoked and watched, and I dreamed that some-day a young man would see me and choose me as his bride." She unfastened her robe. Slowly it settled to the ground in a dark puddle around her feet.

"Nesrin, I don't think…"

She snapped her fingers to a beat only she heard. Tonight she needed no castanets, no flute to carry a melody that was a part of her soul. Her pulse set the tempo. No man had ever chosen her, and the man she would have had denied his love. She would not lie to herself. She could not make Parker love her, any more than she had been able to force her father to grasp the fragile bond of love she had offered him in childish in-nocence.

But here, in the ruins of her past, she could pretend for one night, unfettered by fears that had held her captive for so long.

Beginning slowly, she began to sway. With the circling of her hips, she set the veils of her skirt in motion swirling around her. Bonelessly, her arms imitated the rolling curves of desert dunes stretching to the horizon. Or alternately beckoned to the stars. Her body flowed with feminine knowledge. Of man. Of woman. Of the beginnings of civilization.

By wiles learned artfully nine hundred years ago, Nesrin lured Parker to her. Soon they would partner in a dance as old as time.

"Nesrin . . . you're so damn beautiful." His face glistened with sweat, his eyes filled with desire, and his voice was rough with wanting. "If you keep this up . . . dammit, I can't be responsible . . ."

She spun her spell around the fire. Seducing with her eyes. Enticing with her fluid movements. Until he stood before her.

He groaned as he pulled her into a collision with the hard length of his body. His mouth covered hers. Hot. Achingly passionate. And when she gasped at the fury of his taking, he plunged his tongue inside. She responded with her own murmur of approval. Elation swept through her that his need of her was so great. At this moment, in this place, she willingly accepted the substitute he proffered for the love he could not give. Not forever, she reminded herself. Only for this one night.

She gave herself over to the urgency of her own need. Without guilt, she sought satisfaction.

He pulled her down onto the sleeping blankets that had been stretched beside the fire. "If you want me to stop, say the word," he pleaded even as his hands stripped her of the flimsy costume she wore. "I'll find a way to stop. I swear it."

"I want this as much as you." Perhaps more so, since she realized they would never be together like this again.

His hands were all over her. Hot and stroking. Discovering intimate places she had not realized existed. And his tongue. Praise be! His tongue laved erotically on flesh that yearned for its warm, damp roughness. And then he suckled, deeply drawing her nipples one at a time into the moist cavern of his mouth.

Dimly she realized in this spell, as in all those she cast with her mystical powers, things had gotten out of hand. She was no longer in control and would not have wanted it otherwise. He was magnificent.

When she was breathless and writhing, he rose above her. The star-filled canopy of the night sky outlined his head as he entered her. Possessed her. She shuddered at the impact of his total dominance, and arched up to meet him.

She scored his back with her fingernails, traced the shape of muscles that rippled across his back. Her legs tightened around him. She cried out. She could not escape the tension that built within her, though she struggled for release.

It came in a burst of sweet pleasure.

Parker stroked into her even more heavily. He was irresistible. A moment later his cry of satisfaction lanced out into the vastness of the desert, and in the far distance a wolf howled in answering approval.

Time took on an undefined quality, much as it had during long periods while Nesrin had been in the lamp. But now she felt the comfort of Parker's weight, and his breath rasping moistly against her ear. She drifted.

At some point, she realized he was no longer a part of her, and she moaned in protest. Later she was aware of him covering her with a coarse blanket against the chilling night air.

She nestled into the heat of his body.

Before dawn he took her again. More slowly this time, but with just as much hunger, and a backdrop of stars that had shifted and reformed themselves.

The sun was full up when she awoke.

Parker's side of their makeshift bed was empty. Again.

She mentally cursed in a half-dozen languages. Didn't he realize a woman *liked* waking up in a man's arms?

In that instant, the realization that he could not love her any more than her father had made Nesrin so angry she was ready to spit date pits. What did they think she was? *Chopped lizard?*

She was worth more than that. Much more. And Parker was about to find that out for himself.

Chapter Eleven

Parker studied his reflection in the truck's cracked side mirror and cautiously drew the razor blade across his whiskers. The morning chill gave no hint of the oppressive heat that was to come. Just like he didn't have a clue how a man could tell the difference between love and old-fashioned lust. Assuming there was such a thing as love.

Parker had always been told that showing emotion was a sign of weakness.

A man parachuted into enemy territory without blinking an eye. If you could manage to do it without sweaty palms, so much the better.

Even in peace time, friends died in the military, particularly in an outfit like Special Forces. So you didn't get too close to anyone. You never revealed too much of yourself. That way you didn't become vulnerable.

Emotions were volatile.

They confused the hell out of Parker. So did Nesrin.

She'd touched him in some deep place last night, activated a set of nerve endings that didn't react in a nice, ordered way. For the first time in his life he'd been totally out of control.

He didn't like the feeling.

In the mirror he caught the reflection of Nesrin walking toward him.

As he turned, Nesrin drew in a steadying breath. Valiantly she tried to ignore the fact that he had not yet put on his shirt and wore only khaki pants. She didn't want to think about his bare chest, or the light smattering of curly hair that arrowed beneath his belt.

"Good morning," she said with forced brightness.

His gaze flicked over her, his expression confused then hurt. "You don't have to follow the local custom about being covered from head to toe when we're out here in the middle of nowhere. I like to be able to see you."

"You have never seen me, Parker Dunlap. Not as I really am."

"Honey, I figure I saw all there is of you last night. And I definitely approve."

"Then perhaps this also will please you." She slid her hand into the folds of her skirt. Closing her eyes and concentrating with great care, she produced a mourning dove that perched on her finger. The bird cooed softly.

A smile twitched the corners of Parker's mouth. "A tame bird? Where'd you find him?"

"I conjured him from thin air." With her other hand she delved into her gown to produce a pair of doves. Except three appeared when she held out her arm, each of them scrambling for a secure position. She lofted one into the air.

"Hey, that's impressive."

"Not really. It was one of the first conjuring spells my father taught me. Even a young genie can master this small bit of magic." In this case, with a slip so minor only another genie would know she had erred.

His lips shifted into a grim line. "Nesrin, let's cut the talk about—"

"Perhaps you would care for a whole flock of doves, master. Like the black birds that attacked the wasps at your ranch?"

"You're talking crazy. Maybe it's the water—"

Birds poured from her raised fingertips, lifting into the air with soft, cooing calls, and the whisper of wings. They circled above the truck.

Parker's eyes rounded. "Did you find a set of magic tricks down in that cellar?"

"Would you prefer buzzards? I can produce those, as well."

"No." Sweat beaded his forehead. "Look, why don't we head on back to town? When we get there—"

She produced a levitating ball. The crystal orb spun right in front of Parker's nose.

"Nesrin, what the hell are you doing?"

"Convincing you I am well and truly a genie."

"These are just tricks. You can see them at any magic show in the country."

"Is that so?" She fumed. As a genie she might not be all that skilled, but she had more facility than a simple magician who used sleight of hand to accomplish his tricks.

She focused on Parker's belt buckle. Instantly his belt pulled free from both ends.

He grabbed at his pants. "What the hell? What are you doing?"

"Is that a trick you see every day? Or this?" Their bedding—the coarse blankets on which they had lain together in such ecstasy—flew into the back of the truck. They kept coming nonstop. Red blankets. Blue ones. Plaids and knobby tweeds. Wool. Cotton. Silken coverlets. Until finally Nesrin gave her head a quick shake to stop the spell.

She drew an uneven breath.

"How did you...how did you do that?" he asked, visibly shaken out of his complacency.

"I am a genie, Parker. I was born in this village nine hundred years ago. My father, and his before him, were genies with mystical powers far greater than mine. I was condemned into a lamp, and you, Parker Dunlap, released me."

"No."

"Would you like me to conjure another spell? A thousand wolves, perhaps. Or a sandstorm. I have never tried that." She flicked her wrist and a fountain of sand arose around his feet.

The horrified look in Parker's eyes sent a shaft of pain to Nesrin's heart. Now he believed her. Finally. And the reality appalled him. In his mind, she had become a monstrous witch. She had not anticipated such a disastrous reaction. She had only wanted him to see her...accept her...as she was.

His normally healthy complexion drained of all color, then his cheeks shot through with furious red. "Last night...did you...what we did...was that a spell you cast?"

"Not in the same way," she conceded softly. She had cast that spell with her heart, evidently with even less skill than she could conjure mourning doves into the air.

"The other things...back at the ranch..." She could almost see his memories scrolling through his mind. "Those birds were your doing?"

She nodded.

"At the river, when Kevin said the horse flew?"

"I believe I levitated Magnum without realizing what I was doing. Normally such an act is a very complicated spell to conjure."

Visibly shaken, he said, "Once I saw Amy floating above the bed. Did you—"

"I was practicing. She fell when you broke my concentration."

"Once, I thought...dammit, I was sitting on a throne and eating grapes. Did you..."

She nodded again. "I was not sure you would also see the vision of my mind's eye."

"Good God..." He snatched up the shirt he had hung over the truck's windowsill and tugged it on. "I think we'd better get back to town."

"Yes, of course." Keeping her chin held high, she went around to the passenger side of the truck. Her future now seemed no less bleak than during the long years she had spent in the darkness of the lamp.

He sat there, his knuckles white on the steering wheel. "Maybe it'd be quicker if you just zapped us back to the airport. Or all the way to Colorado, for that matter."

"If you wish, I will attempt such a spell. But you should know my powers are sometimes erratic."

"Are you saying we could end up at the North Pole?"

"Possibly."

With a disbelieving shake of his head, he started the engine. "If you don't mind, I think I'd rather rely on a more ordinary mode of transportation."

As they drove away, Nesrin glanced over her shoulder and directed the full power of her incantations at the ruins.

A moment later there was a gratifying rumble from deep in the earth. A cloud of dust rose from the village as the walls of Rasheyd's evil conjuring room collapsed in on themselves. Above the ground, walls already dissolving to dust toppled over and filled the hole. There was no trace left of the man who had brought Nesrin so many years of agony.

Even so, she felt little sense of relief. Her heart was already filled with too much sorrow that Parker could not love her.

THE TRAFFIC THROUGH TOWN en route to the airport was as chaotic as Parker's thoughts.

A *real* genie? With a bag of tricks that had no logical explanation?

Impossible.

Except he'd seen it with his own eyes. More than once. All the way from the ruins back to the city, incidents had looped through his brain like a circling videotape. A mile-high pile of peanut butter sandwiches. Black birds appearing out of nowhere. A horse that literally flew. And finally a belt and buckle snapping apart for no apparent reason.

Parker's equilibrium shifted. He was spinning on a centrifuge and pulling too many Gs, but he couldn't find the "chicken" switch that would stop the damn thing so he could get off.

A garishly painted taxi darted out from a side street right into his path. Parker swerved the truck just in time to avoid a collision.

Or maybe Nesrin had cast a spell to ward off the vehicle.

How the hell was he supposed to know? It was enough to drive a man crazy.

Worse yet, he wouldn't dare let anyone back home know the truth. The locals would be sure Nesrin was a candidate for the funny farm. Hell, they'd probably escort *both* Nesrin and Parker inside and lock the door. At the very least, they'd turn her into a media sideshow.

Where would any of that leave Amy and Kevin? he wondered in a grim moment of near panic.

With a great gnashing of gears, the truck lurched to a stop in the airport parking lot. Abdel knew to pick it up later and return it to the owner. That had been part of the deal made by the honorable beggar. Parker's job was to get Nesrin safely out of the country without a passport, which was likely to take a lot of smooth talking on his part.

"When we get inside let me handle things," he warned. "You not having a passport is going to make getting a ticket out of the country a little dicey."

As Nesrin got out of the truck, she asked, "When does the plane leave?"

"In less than an hour, if it's on time."

She nodded. Soon she would be leaving her homeland forever. Certainly there was nothing in this harsh country to keep her and she had no doubts Parker would complete what he saw as his duty to her, helping her to escape Rasheyd and his men.

Her future, however, was still obscured by her feelings for Parker.

Although she had grown accustomed to the clothing worn in his country, and the freedom of movement they provided a woman, today she was grateful to be fully veiled. She had held herself erect and determined throughout the entire trip back from her village, but she knew if she were unveiled, her face would reveal a deep sadness that she could not mask.

Walking two paces behind Parker, as was the custom of her people, she followed him toward the bustling air terminal. The modern glass-and-steel building contrasted sharply with the ruins of her ancient village, and the poverty of the beggars who lingered near the entrance. Inside it was like a crowded bazaar. Nesrin closed the gap between herself and Parker. He carried the lamp, with its treasure of jewels, in a pack slung over his shoulder.

Parker glanced over his shoulder. "Can you keep up, Nesrin? I don't want us to get separated in this crowd."

When he reached for her, she shrugged away. "Hush, Parker," she hissed. "You will draw attention to us. I am *supposed* to walk behind you."

He grimaced. "Well, stay close."

But it was already too late. Someone in the crowd had noticed them.

"There she is!" a woman shouted. "Look at her feet! That gold anklet!"

Nesrin whirled. "Tuëma," she gasped. "Rasheyd's wife."

"Get the man, too," a male voice shouted. "The sheikh wants his eyes plucked and mounted. Ten thousand rupees is the reward."

Parker cursed. He grabbed Nesrin's hand and pulled her away from the ticket lines. At a run, they raced back outside.

"Rasheyd wants the gems," Nesrin said. "Give them to him."

"He wants more than that, Nesrin. You can bet he still wants you. Forget he wants to mount my eyeballs for a trophy."

She groaned. Parker was right. She had angered Rasheyd and embarrassed him in front of his friends. He would want vengeance, as well as the gems. Against both of them.

"Then you must go without me. You can catch the plane and I will hide—"

"Not on your life, sweetheart."

"But no one will recognize you."

"Rasheyd and one of his buddies would. They came to the ranch, remember?"

"But not when you were wearing the robes of an Arab."

They raced around the end of the building and stopped, both of them breathing hard. Nesrin knew Parker was trying to form a plan in his mind. Their situation appeared quite hopeless, unless—

Fear sliced through her. Could she, even to save Parker, suggest such a desperate plan? She wanted to be that noble. She wanted to believe her love for him would be strong enough to carry her across a terrible threshold and safely back again.

But nine hundred years of darkness had taken its toll. Her courage faltered.

"Perhaps we could drive the truck to the border," she suggested.

"You're right. That's probably our best bet." He peered around the corner, then swore loudly. "There're guards swarming all over the damn truck. They've got Abdel, too, and it looks like they're having a very *unfriendly* conversation with him."

Tears sprang to Nesrin's eyes. She could not allow Abdel to suffer. Not if she had the power to protect him.

"Parker, you must curse me back into the lamp."

He cut her a glance. "Honey, that kind of stunt is way outside my league."

"I remember the words Rasheyd spoke." If she had been in the lamp ten thousand years, she never would have forgotten a syllable of the ancient words that had condemned her. "If you repeat them after me then I will vanish into the lamp."

"What good will that do us?" Though skeptical, at least he had listened to her idea. "They're still going to nail me."

"The jewels in the lamp will save us. When I am back in the lamp, you will scatter the gems on the ground in front of the building and I will conjure up a hundred more beggars—"

"Can you do that from inside the lamp?"

"I do not know," she conceded. "Even so, I think the plan will work and will solve the problem of my not having a passport, for no one will see me." Surely, though desperate, it was their best chance. And she hated herself that she was so frightened by the prospect. "With so many jewels on the ground, people will go crazy. Then you will slip inside the building and simply become an Arab businessman traveling alone to America."

"Carrying a brass lamp in my hands?"

"Yes, please. I would not wish to remain here." Not in unending darkness so far away from Parker she would not even hear his voice again.

"Has it occurred to you, *if* I can get you inside that lamp, I don't have the vaguest idea of how to get you back out again?"

"You did it before."

"Yeah, but—"

A bloodcurdling scream came from across the parking lot. Abdel...

"There is no time to waste, Parker. Say these words after me."

Nesrin began the curse, slowly, hesitantly, her voice trembling on each harsh sound. As Parker's deep voice echoed hers, dread gnawed through Nesrin's awareness. To never feel the warmth of the sun on her flesh again, nor to see a human face, was a terrible price to pay. But to know she would never feel Parker's arms around her, or his lips pressed against hers once more was almost a greater burden than she could bear.

Abdel screamed anew. She had no choice but to continue. An honorable man, the beggar should not pay that which was still due on her father's wager.

She finished the curse, and so did Parker.

A great pressure squeezed her from all sides. She called out her pain, but to no avail. As she felt her insides reshape and become boneless, she knew it was too late. Her dancing skirt caught on a rough edge, and she knew her only hope was that Parker could recall the power that had once released her from imprisonment.

She trembled in the darkness of the lamp, and a single tear crept down her cheek as she prayed that Parker would remember the key that would allow her escape.

"MY GOD . . . NESRIN?"

The impossibility of what had happened sliced through Parker's gut. There was no longer a way to deny it, no way to rationalize or hedge. *Nesrin was a genie.* And he'd just watched the last trace of her silken skirt vanish into a brass lamp. She was gone. Vanished. The lamp hadn't changed one iota. Not the weight. Not the look of it. Except now Nesrin was inside.

Shock ripped through him like a linebacker hitting a quarterback full on. He all but stumbled backward with the impact.

He looked around as if by still denying what he knew to be true, he could make her reappear, her flesh warm, her dark eyes gleaming with the trick she'd pulled—a magician's assistant who pops up on the opposite side of the stage, to the wild approval of a gullible audience.

But he couldn't make her reappear. Not yet. And the goons were still having a serious conversation with Abdel. He needed a distraction and he needed it now.

He lifted his incredulous gaze from the lamp and found what he'd been hoping for. Scores of beggars milled around the entrance to the air terminal. More beggars than Parker had ever seen in his life, and the number seemed to be growing. Nesrin had done her part by casting a spell. Now it was his turn to get the two of them safely out of the country.

He adjusted his turban lower on his head and checked his robes. A traveling Arab businessman, *if* no one got too close a look.

Heading purposefully toward the mob of beggars, he tipped the lamp. Green and red gems spilled out of the spout into his palm. He hoped it would be equally easy later on to retrieve Nesrin from inside the lamp.

"Here we go," he said to her, feeling foolish talking to a lamp.

He'd taken only a few steps when he spotted the beady eyes and hawk nose of Rasheyd on the opposite side of the mob. Things were likely to get very uncomfortable if Parker didn't act quickly.

He seeded the sidewalk with a handful of gems. "Rubies for the sons of Allah," he announced.

For a moment, he didn't think anyone in the crowd had heard him. The beggars kept milling around hassling anyone who looked as if they might have a few extra coins.

Parker began to sweat. Rasheyd was getting closer. The whole deal was about to blow up in his face. "Nesrin, nothing's happening...."

Then, as though they'd heard a silent command, the mob surged forward like the head of some monstrous dragon. Those in front dived for the gems on the ground. Others shoved their way up from the back of the crowd. They shouted and cursed.

Parker tossed another handful of treasures into the air.

The beggars scrambled for their share, all of them equally greedy. They swarmed past Rasheyd until he was lost in the crowd.

Bystanders raced to join in the hunt. The goons from the parking lot, unwilling to give up the sudden windfall to others without a fight, sprinted to enter the melee, leaving Abdel unattended.

Parker threw more stones into the fray. Then, with the care of a precision quarterback, he tossed the last red ruby in Abdel's direction. It landed at the beggar's feet. Abdel waved his acknowledgment, and Parker figured the old man would make good use of the money the gem would provide. A small token of his appreciation, Parker thought grimly, wishing it would be as easy to save his ranch. But for the moment, escape and Nesrin's safety came first.

Skirting the throng, Parker made his way into the terminal. Travelers and workers alike dashed past him as the word spread about precious gems covering the ground. He could hear fistfights breaking out behind him adding to the general chaos.

He found himself alone at the check-in counter. No clerks. No customers.

Still carrying the brass lamp, he clambered through the counter opening usually reserved for luggage. He spent a hurried minute trying to get the computer to spit out a ticket for him, and then gave it up. He'd have to bluster his way on board.

All of the security personnel, lured by the chance of instant wealth, had abandoned their posts, so Parker didn't have to worry about setting off alarms at the metal detectors with his bum ankle. He simply sauntered around them.

It all seemed too easy. And it was, except for the anxiety that had his heart racing and sweat creeping down his spine. But still no one stopped him as he boarded the waiting plane and settled into a seat in first class.

The corner of his mouth twitched into a troubled grimace. For all he knew, Nesrin was inside the lamp conjuring up spells that would make this 747 fly them back home without the necessity of a pilot. Or else they'd end up at the North Pole.

He cradled the lamp in his arms.

When he got Nesrin back home, she would have to swear off this genie business. It was too damn nerve-racking.

Chapter Twelve

Parker placed the lamp smack in the middle of the back of his pickup. Right where he'd found it the first time. Shivering against the cold blast of morning air that swept down from the Colorado peaks, Parker willed the inanimate brass object to respond to his command.

"Let her go, dammit!"

Parker had racked his brain all the way home from the Middle East trying to remember what he had done that had released Nesrin from her prison. He'd been thinking about Marge . . . and her kids, he recalled. But what had he said or done that had broken a centuries old spell? He'd tried a dozen different ideas and so far had come up empty.

"You're the genie," he pleaded aloud, hoping Nesrin could hear him. "Can't you get yourself out of there?" She should have given him the necessary words before he put her back in there. But then, maybe she didn't know them, either. As near as he could tell, her spells weren't all that precise.

God, she had to be going crazy inside that lamp. He remembered how much she hated the dark and knew what a sacrifice it had been for her to voluntarily reenter that living tomb. He wished he could hold her, reassure her, tell her there wasn't anything about the dark she had to fear.

Where had she found the courage to risk spending eternity inside a dinky little lamp? He'd known men with chests full of medals who weren't half as brave as she was. Himself included.

If he'd thought it would do any good, he'd take a can opener to the lamp and be done with it. He'd get Nesrin out of there. But he didn't think that's how undoing curses worked.

Idly his thumb smoothed over the ancient inscriptions on the lamp and he wished he was stroking Nesrin's soft skin instead.

"I did a lot of thinking on the flight home and I've finally gotten things worked out," he said as he shifted the lamp in his hands. The truck shocks gave a little as Parker rested one hip on the tailgate. A couple of birds were singing their morning greetings, and the bees were busy taste-testing purple lupine that had grown wild at the edge of the grass, but he paid no attention to any of that. "I figure we can get married and that'll more or less take care of the immigration problem. You'll be legal and there won't be too many questions asked." Like date of birth, he thought grimly.

"You won't be able to tell anyone you're a genie, of course," he continued. "That would really gum up the works. You can imagine what the general would make of it in a custody hearing if I announced my wife was a nine-hundred-year-old genie who casts spells as a hobby.''

In spite of himself, Parker chuckled. His dad would have apoplexy at the thought. Nesrin simply didn't fit into any of the old man's neat little niches. Even her spells weren't very well disciplined. It would serve him right if Parker told him the truth.

But he couldn't risk that if it meant he would lose custody of the kids. Maybe later...

''See, I figure if we get married I can watch out for you. Keep you out of trouble, you know?'' He'd always taken on the protector's role. With his sister, Marge. His troops. And now the kids. He'd simply add Nesrin to his responsibilities. From his point of view it made a lot of sense.

''There're a lot of guys out there who would take advantage of your, well, innocence. In fact, if you let it be known you're a genie, there'd be a raft of hotshot promoters who'd want to turn you into a media circus. TV interviews. The press hanging around our front door all the time. You wouldn't like that. It's better if we handle everything low-key. No more genie. No more spells. Just you and me and the kids.''

He looked down at the lamp. It seemed to be growing hotter in his hands by the minute, the metal almost glowing with angry heat.

Now why the hell would that be happening? He was just explaining what needed to be done.

Damn, he wished he could remember what he'd said to get Nesrin out of the lamp. Desperation beaded his forehead with sweat. His gut knotted on a painful possibility he didn't want to admit. What would he do if he couldn't release Nesrin? Ever.

Worse, what would she do?

He must have said or done something simple the first time, he reasoned, damping down an uncharacteristic sense of growing panic. Something he hadn't given any particular thought to. Something easy. Like . . .

His eyes widened.

"Abracadabra!"

She exploded out of the lamp like a comet.

"May all your daughters be toothless and your sons have pointy tails!" Nesrin cried as she burst into being again.

"What?" Parker asked incredulously, both grateful and confused by her acrimonious appearance.

"I would not marry you if you were the last man on earth."

He shook his head. "Why the hell not? We've already slept together—"

"Does that mean you love me?"

"Love doesn't have anything to do with—"

"Then what we did was no more than that which a master would demand of his harem girl."

Her accusation brought him up short. "You know that's not true." Didn't she realize he cared about her? A lot. What they'd done together went a hell of a lot deeper than gratuitous sex.

But how much deeper? asked a niggling voice at the back of Parker's mind.

Before he could respond to the thought, Nesrin continued furiously, "You have never been able to accept me for what I am. A genie. Granted I am not as skilled as some who have gone before me, and sometimes my spells go awry, but I am very likely the only living genie in the entire world. That should stand for something."

"Well, yes, sure." She was in his face and he had no choice but to take a step back. Her expression was as foreboding as the dark robes she wore. He wanted to hold her, hug her, and do a whole lot more. But this didn't seem like the time or place to press the issue. He hadn't realized she had such a fierce temper. It was kind of cute.

"Furthermore, I have no need of a man to take care of me. Tuëma, Rasheyd's wife, settled for that and she is a miserable creature. Angry, greedy and loathsome, interested in gems she did not earn. I am quite capable of caring for myself and I prefer it that way."

"I didn't mean—"

"You think me simpleminded? Capable of no more than conjuring up a few peanut butter sandwiches for your evening meal? Do you not think a genie has feelings, too?"

"Nesrin, you're getting carried away. I never meant to insult you. For God's sake, I just proposed to you."

"Because you thought it your duty." She cocked her head and scowled. "Why is it so quiet?"

Parker had to shift mental gears in order to respond. "The day you were kidnapped someone let the horses out of the corral. I figure it was Rutherford trying to break his contract with me."

She glanced at the nearly empty corral. Only two swayback mares stood in the shade of the barn. "No, it was Rasheyd who let the horses go. He wanted you to go off in search of the horses rather than come after me."

"His plan didn't work. But it looks like Rusty and the boys haven't had much luck rounding the mustangs up again."

"Does this mean you will lose the ranch?"

"Looks like it." He tried to sound casual, but the fact that his dream was coming apart hurt like hell. "At this point, there's not one chance in a thousand I'll have twenty saddle-broken mounts back in the corral by the time I'm due to deliver the goods at the end of the week. I won't get paid and neither will the bank. They'll foreclose."

"Then what will happen to the children? Will your father—"

"I'll fight him every inch of the way." He sucked in his gut as though preparing for a blow to his midsection. That's what losing the kids would feel like. "I may lose the ranch and I won't have any capital left, but I won't be exactly poverty-stricken. I'll get a job in the security business."

"But that is not what you wanted."

"No," he conceded. He didn't want to admit he'd failed again. The military first, and now the ranch, his lifelong dream. Wouldn't his dad just eat that up. His perfect son gone bust. Twice. Maybe he didn't have a right to ask Nesrin to marry him, even as a matter of convenience. She could sure as hell do better than a two-time loser. In fact, if she had good sense she'd walk out on him for sure. Just like his ex.

He cleared the press of failure from his throat, and the memory of a lifetime of not measuring up. "The kids need you, Nesrin. You and I don't have to marry if that's not what you want."

Tears sprang to her eyes. In so many ways he was offering what every woman dreamed of, but offering the dream without the love that was the most important ingredient. As Louanne had said, living with a man without love would be a misery. But the children...dear heaven, Nesrin would miss them. As she would miss Parker.

"There is no need for you to lose the ranch," she said.

"It'll take a miracle to get those horses back in time."

"Or a spell conjured by a genie." She whispered her promise, a gift she alone could bestow on Parker in gratitude for releasing her from the lamp.

"Nesrin, I don't want you to cast any spells to save the ranch. It's un-American."

But she wasn't listening to him and had already closed her eyes. She pictured Lucifer and his harem of brown and mud-colored mares; she spoke from her heart to the magnificent stallion and urged him to return to the ranch. She sensed only she could give Parker what he so desperately needed—the freedom to love—but he had refused that precious gift. A herd of mustangs seemed a poor substitute.

The first indication that something was happening came like the echo of distant thunder rumbling through the mountains. The sound amplified as it grew closer. Soon the ground began to shake. Dust billowed into a cloud. The scent of sweaty horseflesh filled the morning air.

From the roiling dust a stallion trumpeted, and Lucifer burst out of the cloud at the head of his harem.

Dumbfounded, Parker counted the mares. Ten. Twenty. Thirty. Forty. Twice, three times as many as they had previously rounded up. The horses kept coming, circling the barn and corral, stirring the dust into a cloud that rose to block out the blue sky, turning morning to twilight. Fine, powdery dirt filled the air. It settled on Parker's shoulders, and in his hair. He tasted the grit.

As though in response to a signal pitched well above Parker's hearing, the horses stopped their wild circling. They milled around, nibbling on sprigs of grass or reaching through the corral fence to get at leftover hay in the feed trough.

Three more horses galloped into sight.

"Yahoo!" Rusty shouted, waving his hat. He headed for the corral, bent to unlatch the gate. Pete and Buck shooed the horses into the pen. Except for Lucifer, they went easily. The stallion gave one of his mares a last nudge, then turned, reared—his hooves pawing the air as he trumpeted again—and he raced back toward the hills. A few of the mares escaped to follow.

Squaring his hat, Rusty announced, "That was the dernedest thing I ever did see. A few minutes ago we had no more'n a half dozen of them mustangs rounded up. Then they started coming down out of the hills all by theirselves, hell bent to get back here to the corral on their own. I never seen the like.''

Parker shook his head. He felt as though he'd just awakened from a dream. He'd been fighting the nightmare of losing his ranch and maybe the kids. Now he had enough horses to not only fulfill the contract that was due, but to get cash ahead for expansion. He'd be able to buy stock, to take care of overdue maintenance, even buy Amy that pony she was so anxious to have. All because Nesrin had cast up one of her spells, he realized—a spell to save the ranch for him.

Smiling, he turned to thank her.

She wasn't there.

The brass lamp still rested on the truck's tailgate where he'd left it, but there was no sign of Nesrin.

No footprints in the dust. No scrap of colorful silk dangling from the lip of the lamp.

She'd vanished into the cloud of dust as though she had never existed at all.

Something inside Parker's chest cracked, like cement struck with a sledgehammer, and he almost cried aloud at the raw agony. He knew he wasn't capable of love, not with the upbringing he'd had. But if he were, he imagined the emotion couldn't be any more painful than what he was experiencing right now.

NESRIN WATCHED from a hidden spot as Parker picked up the children from Louanne's house. She had known he would come for them. Now a part of her wanted to run to him, to tell him she would be his harem girl, if that was all he wanted of her. But nine hundred years of pride held her immobile.

If she had been willing to settle for so little in life, she would have submitted to Rasheyd's demands centuries ago, and avoided all of those painful years imprisoned in the lamp. To acquiesce now would mean her suffering had meant nothing.

Tears edged down her cheeks.

She still loved Parker. Nothing would change that. But she would not give herself to him if he could not return that love.

Cautiously she made her way to Louanne's and tapped lightly on the door.

"Well, land's sake, Nesrin, honey. What are you doing here?"

"I had nowhere else to go," she admitted. Without a single rupee to her name, and only the clothes she wore, Nesrin desperately needed a friend.

"Well, come on in and I'll give Parker a call." She opened the door wide and Nesrin followed her into the kitchen. "He hasn't been gone but a minute or two."

"No, you must not tell him I am here."

Louanne tilted her head to study Nesrin more carefully. "You two young folks have yourselves a lovers' spat?"

"He does not love me."

"That so? He sure was fit to be tied, pacing and carrying on like a wild man. Said you'd plum vanished, right when a whole herd of them mustangs came galloping back from the hills."

"He only wants me because of the children. To help with their care." He could not accept her as she was any more than her father had been able to.

"That a fact?" Louanne pulled out a chair at the kitchen table and nodded for Nesrin to sit down.

"From what I've seen I reckon that young man's already toppled head over heels for you. What he most likely needs is a good dose of competition to make him take a real good look at himself and come to his senses. Men sometimes need a little nudge to see things straight. I know all three of my husbands did." She patted Nesrin on the shoulder. "If I can come up with a plan that will get his attention, you willing to give it a shot?"

"I would do anything if it would mean Parker would love me."

"Good girl."

Louanne sat down and the two of them put their heads together. Nesrin grinned as the plan unfolded and her hopes grew. Perhaps there was yet a way she could capture Parker's love and be able to hold it as her own.

ABRACADABRA! Parker pounded his fist on the mantel, making the lamp jump.

"What are you doing, Uncle Parker?"

He whirled around. "Nothing, son." Except he was nearly hoarse from shouting at the damn lamp for the past three days. He'd looked everywhere else he could think of and still no sign of Nesrin.

"I sure miss Nesrin," Kevin said. "I wish she'd come back."

"Yeah, so do I, kid. So do I."

"That Mr. Mildon is here to pick up the horses, Uncle Parker."

"Okay. I'm coming." He shot a final look at the lamp. Where the hell could Nesrin have gone?

Rutherford was waiting for him at the corral.

"I admit, Parker, I didn't think you'd be able to make delivery," he said as he handed over the check for the mares. "'Specially when I heard you'd lost most of the herd."

"Yeah, and I bet you were chuckling up your sleeve when you thought you'd be able to break our contract, and save yourself a bundle in the process."

Rutherford's face went red, and his jowls formed a second double chin. "Now don't you go accusing me of something you cain't prove, boy."

"I'm not. And since you've got your horses and I've got your check, it doesn't matter now."

"Now look here, young man. I only heard about your troubles at the High Mountain Saloon last night. I was watchin' that pretty little lady of yours sashaying around on that stage, when old Jeb Dobson said something about—"

"What pretty little lady?"

"That there wisp of a girl I saw you with at the grocery store a few weeks back. She's a knockout. And ooo-eee, can she ever shake it like nobody I ever saw before."

Parker couldn't get rid of Rutherford fast enough. Nesrin was at the saloon. Dancing! Probably in that little skimpy costume.

God, didn't she know those rough-and-tumble cowboys who frequented the place would make mincemeat of her?

He was going to get her out of there. Back to the ranch where she belonged. Dammit, it was his *duty* to take care of her.

He'd been glad enough to see his ex leave. But that wasn't the case with Nesrin. He missed her like hell and there was no way he was going to let her simply walk out on him . . . and the kids, he added as an afterthought. They deserved better, and so did he.

He waited until the kids were in bed, then left Rusty in charge of baby-sitting duty.

Trying to act casual, he sauntered into the saloon. She was dancing. Through the screen of smoke she looked like a slightly out-of-focus dream, and so achingly beautiful Parker wondered if he could grasp her any more tightly than a man could catch the mist that sometimes rose from a winter pond in the high mountains.

As she gyrated on the small dance floor to the canned music of quarter-tone melodies, the murmur of approval rose several decibels. Parker's teeth clenched until his jaw throbbed to the Middle Eastern beat. To his surprise, the cowboys in the bar weren't hootin' and hollerin' as he had expected.

They were in awe of Nesrin. Dammit all, half of them were in sappy, cow-eyed *love* with her, he realized.

He wanted to toss Nesrin over his shoulder and haul her back to the ranch without any debate. But he fig-

ured he'd get quite an argument from fifty or so cowboys if he tried that stunt while she was dancing.

So he waited by the bar, sipping a beer, a jealous rage
burning his gut every time Nesrin smiled that sweet, innocent smile at one of the cowboys up front.

Finally she finished her number to a huge round of
applause. Parker followed her backstage. Or at least he
tried to.

"Where do you think you're going?"

The burly bouncer for the High Mountain Saloon
blocked the hallway to the back of the building. He
looked like he used to be a lineman for the Denver
Broncos and was definitely not a guy Parker wanted to
argue with.

"Nesrin's a friend of mine," he said.

"Yours and every other cowboy who's got the hots
for her. Which includes just about every male in the
county over the age of fifteen. So why don't you move
on back to the bar and have another beer."

A red haze threatened to stifle Parker's better judg-
ment. His fingers flexed into fists. "She'll see me."

"Leave your name. I'll tell her you stopped by to say
hello."

A door opened at the end of the hall. "Is there
something wrong, Roger?"

Roger? It figured.

"Not a thing, Miss Nesrin. I'm just politely asking
this gentleman to leave."

A sheer robe was belted around Nesrin's waist and
her dark eyes flicked coolly over Parker without a spark
of recognition. "What was it he wanted, Roger?"

"He didn't exactly say."

"I want you to get dressed and come home with me," Parker said, his temper rising toward a dangerous peak.

"Why would I want to do a thing like that?" she asked.

"Yeah, why?" Roger echoed. He folded his arms across his massive chest.

"Come on, Nesrin. The kids are asking for you. Amy's been down in the dumps and Kevin crashed the hard disk on my computer. They need you."

"And you want a free baby-sitter? Is that why you want me to return to the ranch?"

"No, that's not what I want." Talking around Roger's hulking form was like talking around a bulldozer.

"You said they needed me before I left," Nesrin reminded him, "and still I went away. What has changed, Parker?"

"Nothing, dammit! I just don't want you working in this dive, understand?"

Roger glared at Parker as though he'd personally affronted the man's place of employment. Which he had.

"I have to support myself," Nesrin said. "In this century women are free to work for a living."

"You don't have to do that. I offered to marry you, didn't I? The ranch is secure now, thanks to you. Rutherford paid me in full. I'm going to sell off the extra mustangs and expand the ranch with good breeding animals. I'm perfectly willing to take care of you. What more do you want?"

"When you learn the answer to that question, please let me know." She turned and vanished behind the closed door of her dressing room.

"Nesrin! I chased halfway around the world for you. You can't—"

"You heard the lady." Roger planted his mountainous body in Parker's path. "She's all done talking, cowboy. Now...clear out."

Parker's jaw clamped down like a tight cork on his temper. He figured he could take this guy, in spite of his size. But what would that get him? If he forced Nesrin to come back to the ranch with him, she'd just leave again. Deep down in his gut he wanted her to come willingly...both back to the ranch and back to his bed.

"I'll be back," Parker warned. "And one of these days we might have to find out just how tough you really are."

"It'd be my pleasure, cowboy."

FIGHTING TEARS, Nesrin hugged herself and leaned back against the closed door of her dressing room. Amy and Kevin did need her. Though Parker was a good man, he was too stern for the children and needed the gentling influence of a woman.

Louanne had assured Nesrin it would not take Parker long to recognize that he loved her. She hoped that knowledge would come quickly. Already she could feel herself weakening. Soon she would be willing to settle for only a kind word from him instead of the love she sought.

Perhaps if she were able to see the children regularly she would be able to endure the loneliness more easily. Louanne could arrange that, and the children could keep their visits a secret.

Then only at night would Nesrin be haunted by memories of Parker's deep, hungry kisses that no amount of determination seemed to erase.

Chapter Thirteen

"I'll be flying into Colorado Springs tomorrow."

Parker's fingers tightened around the phone and a knot formed in his gut. "That's fine, Dad. You want me to pick you up?"

"No, that won't be necessary. I've arranged my own transportation."

"Okay, then I'll see you when you get to the ranch."

"I'm looking forward to seeing the children. We'll talk tomorrow about the arrangements I've made for them."

"They're pretty happy with things right now, sir." A lot more happy than Parker was at this point.

After he hung up, Parker speared his fingers through his hair. He hadn't been able to think straight, not since he discovered a week ago that Nesrin was working in a saloon—her dancing the artistic success of the century, according to the local Gunnison paper. Hell, single-handedly she'd turned the High Mountain Saloon into a cultural mecca. Half the women in town had taken a sudden interest in belly-dancing classes at the local recreation center. It was all the rage.

As he had every night for the past week, Parker climbed into his truck and drove into town. He sidled up to the bar, drank a beer and watched Nesrin dance, all the time hating that other men were watching her, too.

Damn their admiration and respect.

He wanted her to dance only for him. To sway her hips and give him that soft, alluring smile where no one else could see her. And he wanted her back in his bed. Wanted it so much he ached with the need for her.

He remembered how she'd been that night in the desert. Seductive. Instigating their lovemaking. Taking him to heights of passion he hadn't imagined possible, and certainly had never experienced with any another woman.

Then all hell had broken loose the next morning with doves flying everywhere, and he discovered he had a real live genie on his hands. Little wonder he'd felt disoriented.

What he couldn't figure was why she had run away from him when they got back to Colorado, and then gone only as far as Gunnison.

In fact, he'd learned Nesrin was staying at Louanne's, and his cowhands were sneaking the kids over to visit almost every afternoon. But he hadn't let on he'd learned their secret.

So Nesrin still cared about the kids. It was only Parker she didn't want to be around.

And that hurt. Down deep in his gut.

By now he knew her dancing routine by heart, including when she was about to end her number, so before the applause stopped, he beat her to the door leading to her dressing room. He caught her by the arm. Her skin was slick with perspiration. And soft. So soft.

Unsurprised, she looked up at him with those big brown eyes. "What is it you want, Parker?"

"You known damn well what I want. For you to come back to the ranch with me."

"Why? Has something changed since you asked me last night?"

"Yeah. I'm another day older."

She smiled sadly. "You look tired." Her fingertips brushed his cheek in a touch so light it was like a wisp of imagination.

How he ached to feel her touch him like that all over his tired body, stroke him, smooth the weariness from both his muscles and his soul.

"I'm still breaking horses." His voice cracked on his desperate need. "I think I spent more time on the ground today than I did in the saddle."

"I'm sorry."

"My father's coming into town tomorrow."

She paled. "Will he take the children?"

"Not unless he brings an entire army with him."

"Miss Nesrin, you want me to show this cowboy to the exit?" Roger planted his bulk protectively next to Nesrin.

She hesitated for just a heartbeat, long enough for Parker to hope she might have decided to go home with him. Then she shook her head. The strange sadness in her eyes looked as ancient as Parker's bruised body felt.

"Mr. Dunlap was just leaving," she announced in a near whisper. Turning, she walked away, her silk skirt swaying like a colorful rainbow in the dimly lit hallway.

It would have given Parker a great deal of satisfaction to wipe Roger's smug expression from his face with a solid punch to his midsection, but he couldn't get past the sorrow in Nesrin's eyes.

Feeling alone, exhausted and confused, he went home, excused Rusty from his nightly baby-sitting duties and went to bed. He tossed and turned the rest of the night. Maybe a man simply wasn't meant to understand what was going on in the head of a genie.

She knew he couldn't offer her love.

A good home. His protection. But not love. After all, he could hardly give what he had never received.

And hell, he didn't care if she was a genie. That shouldn't have even been an issue.

But Nesrin thought it was, he realized with a start that made him sit upright in bed, the tangle of blankets around his waist. All she'd asked of him was to accept her as she was. In response, he'd told her to keep her wizardry a secret.

No wonder she was mad at him.

After Parker dealt with his father tomorrow, he'd have another talk with Nesrin. This time, he vowed, she'd come back to the ranch with him.

"KEVIN, PUT ON SOME clean pants," Parker ordered, confronting his nephew in the upstairs hallway. "And when you do, tuck in your shirt. Those jeans look like Goodwill rejects."

"They're what I wear every day. I don't see why we have to get all dressed up just because—"

"Out of respect, that's why." Parker turned to Amy. "Where are your shoes, honey?"

"I can only find one." She held up a white dressy shoe by the strap. In her frilly dress, she looked ready for Easter. Unfortunately, Parker hadn't had a chance to comb her hair yet and it was a tousled mess of blond curls. "Besides, these shoes hurt my feet," she whined. "They're too small."

"They're fine. Go look in your closet again," he said. "The other shoe's got to be there somewhere. I don't want you wearing tennis shoes with that dress."

With a pouty lower lip, Amy stalked away.

"What's the big deal?" Kevin protested. "It's just Grandpa."

"Yeah, and the general likes his troops ready for inspection. Did you clean up your room like I told you to?"

"I suppose." Jamming his hands into his pockets, Kevin shuffled off toward his room. The tips of his shoelaces clicked on the hardwood floor at every step.

Parker rolled his eyes. This was going to be a disaster.

He hated that the need for his father's approval still had him jumping through hoops. Now the kids were in the thick of it, too. Well, he didn't care if Kevin didn't like to wear clean clothes, and Amy had to squeeze her feet into shoes two sizes too small. It was only for the day. And Parker wasn't about to give his father any ammunition to challenge his guardianship of the kids.

At the first sound of an approaching car, Parker straightened his spine and went out the door.

A black limousine with a two-star general's pendant flying at the fenders pulled to a stop in front of the porch. A staff sergeant climbed out from behind the wheel and came around to open the door for the passenger. The general was in full dress uniform. He placed his cap squarely on his head, tugging the brim to check the fit.

Parker shook hands with his father, then tipped his head toward the official car. "I thought you'd retired."

"Old habits die hard. And there are still some perks." General Everett Dunlap looked fit and nowhere near his sixty-five years. His back was ramrod straight, his gut tucked in. Only his gray sideburns gave his age away.

In a single critical sweep, the general scanned the ranch house and the outbuildings. Parker knew what he was seeing—a farmhouse and garden that were run-down, and peeling paint on the barn. With money tight, superficial upkeep hadn't been his priority. Now it was enough to be debt free—courtesy of Nesrin, he realized—and building his stock. Though it might not look like it at the moment, he was well on his way to making a success of the ranch. His dream was coming true.

Without the woman who had made it possible.

Regret sliced through Parker like a steel bayonet.

The trio of hired hands puttered nonchalantly in the vicinity of the corral, getting an eyeful of the visiting brass.

"Look's like your troops could use a little more spit and polish, son," the general commented.

Parker bit back a sharp reply. The general's line of command didn't extend as far as Rusty and his cohorts.

"Come on in, Dad. The kids are anxious to see you."

"As I am to see them. It's been a long time."

Kevin, still wearing his ratty jeans but with his shirt tucked in, met them at the top of the steps. "Hi, Grandpa."

Shaking hands with his grandson, the general looked him over with the same critical eye as he had taken in the run-down ranch. "You'll do, young man. *After* a haircut and a little sprucing up, that is."

"Kevin likes comfortable clothes," Parker said, automatically coming to his nephew's defense.

The general harrumphed. "I've got a prep school in mind where he'll learn about spit and polish. Yes, sir. Strictly military. A fine record. Nearly ninety percent of their graduates go on to a military academy. They'll have Kevin primed and ready for West Point in no time at all."

Kevin shot a troubled glance at Parker, then back to the general. "I'm not gonna go to West Point, man. No way. I'm gonna go to M.I.T. They've got the best robotics program in the whole country."

Everett Dunlap let his hands drop to his side and drew himself to rigid attention. "Nonsense, boy. All the

Dunlap men since before the Civil War have been West Point graduates. Our duty to God and country have come first. We'll have no more talk about—"

"I'm not a Dunlap, sir. I'm a Johnson, just like my dad. He said I could go to any school I wanted." Kevin lifted his chin proudly, with an added touch of arrogance that comes with youth.

Parker looped his arm around Kevin's shoulders and gave him a squeeze. "Kevin's a pretty smart kid, Dad, and an absolute whiz with computers. I think when the time comes he'll be able to make the decision about college for himself."

Kevin seemed to grow about an inch as he straightened from his usual slouch.

Meanwhile, the general gave Parker a look as if he were about to order him to clean every latrine in a four-state area—with a toothbrush.

Years of resentment for that kind of treatment strengthened Parker's resolve. He wasn't about to work off any more demerits for his dad. They'd finish with all of that right here on his front porch. Now.

"Kevin, why don't you go see what Rusty is up to over at the corral?" Parker said.

The boy looked up at him. "That means you and Grandpa want to talk grown-up talk, right?"

"You got it, son."

When Kevin was out of earshot, the general said, "Just as well you sent the boy away, because I'm not at all pleased with your attitude. I'm your father and I demand your respect."

A shocking realization struck Parker like lightning strikes a mountain peak. "Dad, you've never really been my father. You've been my *commanding officer,* and in case you haven't already guessed, I'm no longer taking orders from you."

The general looked nonplussed. "Are you saying I wasn't a good father?"

"I'm saying it no longer matters. Marge wanted me to raise her kids if something happened to her, and that's how it's going to be. I'll fight you in every court in the country, if need be, but I won't let you have them and I won't let you send Kevin to any school he doesn't want to go to."

The general's shoulders slumped. Even some of the rigid set to his jaw relaxed. "Do you remember your Grandfather Dunlap?" he asked.

"Vaguely," Parker conceded, puzzled by a question that seemed oddly out of context.

"He was a stern man, even for that day and age. He used to beat me with a cane whenever . . ." Clearing his throat, General Everett Dunlap took off his gold-braided cap and ran his palm across the stubble of thinning gray hair on his head. His age-spotted hand trembled. "I tried to be a better father than that, son. Never once did I raise my hand to you or your sister. Never once."

It had never occurred to Parker that his father had learned to be a parent at the feet of a man who was actually physically abusive—that his father had thought strict discipline without using a cane was an improvement over how he had been raised. In a way, Parker supposed that was true.

But it was another bit of evidence proving Dunlap men weren't capable of love.

That painful thought stuck in his brain in the same way a chicken bone could get lodged in a guy's throat. He worked at it a minute, trying to dislodge the damn thing, and then he realized it was a lie—one he'd allowed to take over his subconscious years ago.

Of course he was capable of love!

Parker had always loved his sister. And he sure as hell loved Kevin and Amy. The feeling might have crept up on him when he wasn't looking, but he loved them so much he'd been willing to challenge his father for their guardianship. In fact, for all these years his father's approval had been important to Parker *because* he loved his dad. In spite of everything.

In a swift mental leap of faith, as though a great weight had been lifted from his psyche, Parker realized he was also capable of loving a woman—Nesrin.

She'd been trying to tell him that all along and he'd been such a knuckleheaded fool he hadn't been listening. In fact, with her quick smile and her open heart, she was the one who had shown him how to love.

He sure as hell hoped she hadn't given up on him yet.

Parker placed a reassuring hand on his father's shoulder. "Come on inside, Dad. I'll get you a beer. I think you and I have a lot of talking to do. Man to man."

Amy picked that moment to come running out of the house, her hair bow askew and wearing only one shoe. She launched herself into Parker's arms. No military machine in the world could have resisted her assault. Certainly not Parker.

He grinned. He could hardly wait to tell Nesrin how much he loved her.

As NESRIN DANCED, tears blurred her vision. A week now, and with each passing day it became more and more obvious her dream that Parker could love her was drying to dust like dates left too long on the tree.

Perhaps she should move away, far enough so that her memories of him would ease with time. She could find a new job, too. Surely there would be a family eager to hire a skilled cook whose specialty was sheep brains mixed with dates.

She sighed.

Even as her hands moved in rhythm to the music, and her hips undulated, she imagined she saw Parker take a seat at one of the front tables. She knew that couldn't be true. He always remained at the bar as he watched her. Silent. Unsmiling. His heart unmoved, turned to stiff leather as though mummified in his chest by a dry, loveless youth.

Now he grinned at her foolishly, and her heart did a wild gyration when she realized he was really there.

"Cast me a spell, genie." His words were softly spoken, but she heard every syllable, and his eyes were dark with promise. Within his words she recognized he accepted her for what she was. And even celebrated the knowledge of her skills.

"What sort of a spell should I cast, master?" she asked, joyously tilting her head and tossing her hair back over her shoulder. She knew something had changed, though she wasn't yet sure what it might be.

"Something that gets us out of here where we can be alone."

With a seductive smile, she rotated her hips and rippled the muscles of her stomach. She flexed her shoulders. A visible sheen of sweat appeared on Parker's forehead. He was aroused, and so was she. But to what purpose?

"Between us, you have always had the greater power, Parker Dunlap. *You* cast the spell."

He rose and moved toward her. Slowly. Purposefully.

She licked her lips, even while she felt the beat of the music throbbing low in her body.

The cowboys sitting near the dance floor quieted, as if they, too, understood the import of Parker's presence.

"I want you to come home with me, genie."

"Why?" She echoed the question that had haunted them both.

He caught her arm, so sweet in his gentle caress. "Because you have taught me to love, Nesrin. I didn't think I could until you showed me how. Please come home with me."

She slid into his embrace. "Kiss me, Parker. Cast us a spell that takes us away from this place. You alone are the most powerful wizard of all."

His lips crossed hers and she was transported. Beyond the bar and the cowboys watching mesmerized, beyond the ragged peaks of the Rockies. His tongue teased with hers, hot and hungry. A cool mountain breeze fanned her heated flesh. She was in a timeless warp. Centuries became insignificant. Time had no meaning.

When she opened her eyes they were alone under the dome of a clear, starlit sky, somewhere between the earth and the heavens above.

"Do you truly love me?" she asked breathlessly.

"More than life itself." Parker pulled her tight into his arms. He'd been searching for Nesrin all of his life. From this moment forward he would never let her go.

He claimed her mouth again in an incantation of love, and they materialized in some magic place. Flesh pressed against flesh, hot and needy, floating through time and space with the power of their combined wizardry. In roughly whispered words of lust and love, Parker cast his spell over Nesrin, binding her to him through eternity, and beyond. Fears vanished. Love grew and expanded to encompass the enchanted landscape.

Together they tumbled past the planets, and when they settled gently back to earth they were wrapped in each other's arms. The light that needed no wick cast a warm golden glow across Parker's bed. The soft cooing sound of dozens of white mourning doves filled the room, the gentle call of lovebirds who had at last found happiness.

Nesrin smiled. Parker Dunlap was indeed a powerful wizard to have cast such a spell. To him she would joyously submit each day... and each night—as long as he agreed to do some submitting of his own.

Once in a while, there's a story so special, a story so unusual,
that your pulse races, your blood rushes. We call this

HART'S DREAM is one such story.

*At first they were dreams—strangely erotic. Then visions—strikingly real. Ever
since his accident, when Dr. Sara Carr's sweet voice was his only lifeline, Daniel Hart
couldn't get the woman off his mind. Months later it was more than a figment
of his imagination calling to him, luring him, doing things to him that only a
flesh-and-blood woman could.... But Sara was nowhere to be found....*

#589 HART'S DREAM
by
Mary Anne Wilson

Available in July wherever Harlequin books are sold. Watch for more Heartbeat
stories, coming your way—only from American Romance!

MILLION DOLLAR SWEEPSTAKES (III)

No purchase necessary. To enter, follow the directions published. Method of entry may vary. For eligibility, entries must be received no later than March 31, 1996. No liability is assumed for printing errors, lost, late or misdirected entries. Odds of winning are determined by the number of eligible entries distributed and received. Prizewinners will be determined no later than June 30, 1996.

Sweepstakes open to residents of the U.S. (except Puerto Rico), Canada, Europe and Taiwan who are 18 years of age or older. All applicable laws and regulations apply. Sweepstakes offer void wherever prohibited by law. Values of all prizes are in U.S. currency. This sweepstakes is presented by Torstar Corp., its subsidiaries and affiliates, in conjunction with book, merchandise and/or product offerings. For a copy of the Official Rules send a self-addressed, stamped envelope (WA residents need not affix return postage) to: MILLION DOLLAR SWEEPSTAKES (III) Rules, P.O. Box 4573, Blair, NE 68009, USA.

EXTRA BONUS PRIZE DRAWING

No purchase necessary. The Extra Bonus Prize will be awarded in a random drawing to be conducted no later than 5/30/96 from among all entries received. To qualify, entries must be received by 3/31/96 and comply with published directions. Drawing open to residents of the U.S. (except Puerto Rico), Canada, Europe and Taiwan who are 18 years of age or older. All applicable laws and regulations apply; offer void wherever prohibited by law. Odds of winning are dependent upon number of eligibile entries received. Prize is valued in U.S. currency. The offer is presented by Torstar Corp., its subsidiaries and affiliates in conjunction with book, merchandise and/or product offering. For a copy of the Official Rules governing this sweepstakes, send a self-addressed, stamped envelope (WA residents need not affix return postage) to: Extra Bonus Prize Drawing Rules, P.O. Box 4590, Blair, NE 68009, USA.

SWP-H595

In June, get ready for thrilling romances and FREE BOOKS—Western-style—with...

WESTERN *Lovers*

You can receive the first 2 Western Lovers titles FREE!

June 1995 brings Harlequin and Silhouette's WESTERN LOVERS series, which combines larger-than-life love stories set in the American West! And WESTERN LOVERS brings you stories with your favorite themes... "Ranch Rogues," "Hitched In Haste," "Ranchin' Dads," "Reunited Hearts" the packaging on each book highlights the popular theme found in each WESTERN LOVERS story!

And in June, when you buy either of the Men Made In America titles, you will receive a WESTERN LOVERS title absolutely FREE! Look for these fabulous combinations:

♦ Buy ALL IN THE FAMILY
by Heather Graham Pozzessere (Men Made In America) and receive a FREE copy of
BETRAYED BY LOVE by Diana Palmer
(Western Lovers)

♦ Buy THE WAITING GAME
by Jayne Ann Krentz (Men Made In America) and receive a FREE copy of
IN A CLASS BY HIMSELF by JoAnn Ross
(Western Lovers)

Look for the special, extra-value shrink-wrapped packages at your favorite retail outlet!

HARLEQUIN®   *Silhouette*®

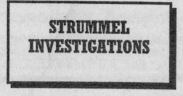

Announcing
the New **Pages & Privileges**™ Program
from Harlequin® and Silhouette®

Get All This FREE
With Just One Proof-of-Purchase!

- **FREE Hotel Discounts** of up to 60% off at leading hotels in the U.S., Canada and Europe

- **FREE Travel Service** with the guaranteed lowest available airfares plus 5% cash back on every ticket

- **FREE $25 Travel Voucher** to use on any ticket on any airline booked through our Travel Service

- **FREE Petite Parfumerie** collection (a $50 Retail value)

- **FREE Insider Tips Letter** full of fascinating information and hot sneak previews of upcoming books

- **FREE Mystery Gift** (if you enroll before June 15/95)

And there are more great gifts and benefits to come!
Enroll today and become Privileged!

(see insert for details)

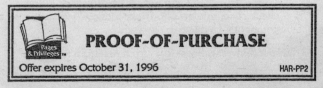

PROOF-OF-PURCHASE

Offer expires October 31, 1996   HAR-PP2